SPEAR SONG

THE ISLE OF DESTINY SERIES BOOK 3

TRICIA O'MALLEY

LOVEWRITE PUBLISHING

FOR THOSE WHO LOOK FOR THE LIGHT.

"Beware of the mermaids, with their hair of rainbow, their eyes of indigo." –
Conny Cernik

CHAPTER 1

"$\mathcal{B}$e still, mother, just now. Just for a moment, now. That's it, love, open your mouth," Lochlain crooned, tilting his mother's head back as he poured another elixir down her throat. It was the fifth carefully-curated potion he'd used just this day and, to his dismay, none of his tinctures were reversing the spell which was slowly murdering his mother from the inside out.

"May the lot of you rot forever in darkness, Domnua," Loch hissed, turning to pace the room as he raked a hand through dark hair that tumbled around a sharply angled face. His golden eyes all but glowed in rage as he continued to curse, his mind racing through the last of the magicks he could possibly perform to save his mother's life.

It had been three days since she'd encountered a Domnua on a foraging excursion deep in the isolated hills of western Ireland. As usual, she'd been harvesting ingredients for her spells that called for being plucked beneath the pale light of a new moon. It was also when the walls between the worlds were thin.

Too thin, as Loch had unfortunately learned. The infamous curse, which had kept the Danula safe and the Domnua banished to the underworld for centuries, was coming to its final days. As the clock ticked on, the Domnua flexed their power, slipping more easily into modern-day Ireland, shielding themselves as they began to enjoy the virtual playground humans provided for them.

The fae – both good and bad – could never resist the fallacies and dramas that came with the human condition. An extended lifespan could do that to a soul, causing the fae to be drawn to the resilient spirit of the humans, endlessly fascinated by watching both wars and love stories unfold.

Once the Domnua had begun to taste their freedom again, keeping them contained had been like trying to hold two hands over a fire hose – they practically poured through the thin veil that separated the worlds. Loch's mother should have known better; he'd warned her, hadn't he? Loch cursed again as his eyes strayed to where she lay on her side, curled beneath a blanket, the fire snapping away to provide additional warmth on this chilly spring day.

There'd been no reason to hurt her – aside from sending a message. Loch had heard tell of it across Ireland, whispered conversations in pubs and snippets of tales from travelers. The Domnua wanted to show they weren't scared, which meant trying to kill the innocents. And had his mother not been as high up in the fae world as she was – a venerable priestess at that – she'd be dead now. Her magick had saved her, but now Loch had to wonder if it was only prolonging a painful end. Coming to his knees at her side, he pressed a hand to her cheek.

"My mother, my heart, I will find your cure. This I promise." Loch pressed his lips to her forehead.

"My son. My heart. If I must go... I must go. My own fault." Her words trailed off, and Loch's heart skipped as he waited for her to take a staggered breath.

"'Tis not your fault, mother, 'tis the murdering Domnua. I will avenge this. But first, I must be off to find you help. I've exhausted my remedies."

"My child. My stubborn, beautiful son. You have such good in you. Don't let the dark win." Her words faded, and Loch wondered if there was a hidden meaning to them. He had no time to waste, though, and brushed his lips over her forehead once more, promising a swift return. Then he rushed from their home with but one destination in mind.

Loch raced through the mists of the early morning, which clung to the moody hedges and rolling hills that sheltered a town that was not known to mortal men. Any human passerby would simply see an expanse of barren hills, but if they were to attempt to climb or explore, they'd be met with a tangled hedge so impenetrable that they would be forced to turn back. His village of magickal people, the Danula, had a stronghold here – one of many scattered throughout Ireland. And far deeper within those hills was a sacred cave of such legend and enchantment that no fae dared go there, as the penalty was death.

Loch paused as he drew near. He felt the press of magick, the invisible barrier of the first ward that would alert to movement near the cave, and stopped just short of it. Reaching out with his extra senses, Loch began to track and find where the various wards and enchantments were. Reaching deep within to magicks he was sworn to never use, Loch began to invalidate and null the wards, spinning quickly through each boundary, firing off spells and magicks until he stood in front of the cave, his heart racing.

If he stepped through this door, his life would be forfeit.

But his mother would live.

Without a second thought, Loch pushed through the door and rushed to find the one thing he knew would save his mother – a bottle of sacred blood from the Goddess Danu herself. Not needing light to see – his eyes adjusted quickly – he raced through the rooms, assessing and discarding all the various treasures found there. Had he more time, he'd allow himself the joy of sifting through the beauty of what was a veritable Aladdin's cave, but every second counted.

Both for his own life and his mother's.

Loch drew to a stop, having rounded a narrow rocky outcropping to find what he sought: a blown glass bottle, twisted and turned in a gossamer-thin veil of faintly purple crystal, vines reaching toward petals containing a Celtic quaternary knot. The stopper itself was a ruby rose of purest red, mirroring the liquid it contained within.

For one infinitesimal moment, Loch's heart stopped as he allowed the sacred beauty of something only whispered about in legends to wash over him, before he shut his thoughts and his fears down. At this point, he was a warrior with one goal in mind – get the magick to his mother. Reaching out, he wrapped his hands around the bottle and tugged it gently from the stand on which it was nestled.

Instantly, light – a thousand times as bright as the stars – lit the room, blinding him, as the sound of the Mireesi, the goddess's avenging angels, raged through the cave, their sound as beautiful as it was painful. It ravaged through his head like millions of razor blades slicing his mind. Before the song made him lose his mind, as it was sure to do, Loch pulled out the last trick he had and vanished into thin air as the angelic warriors flooded the protected space – only to find an empty room with the most sacred of blood missing.

As their cries of despair rolled across the land, those in the village froze, knowing there was a breach, knowing that a death of one of their own was imminent. All eyes turned towards the hills, where a flood of amethyst warriors, winged beasts of the most glorious creation, rolled on molten waves as they poured from every crevice in the hills, madly searching for the one – the only fae in all of time – who had been powerful enough to breach their wards.

And to ensure his death was immediate.

CHAPTER 2

*L*och materialized at his mother's side, wincing as he watched her chest heave, the dreaded death rattle already taking over her withered body. Without hesitation, he pulled the rose stopper from the bottle and gently cupped his mother's chin, pushing her mouth open.

His mother's eyes slitted open, the light in them already fading as she focused on the bottle he held in his hands.

"No…" It was no more than a gasp, a breath of air, but the terror in her eyes was real. She knew as well as any that Loch's actions were a death sentence for him.

"Yes," Loch said. He poured only a few drops into his mother's mouth, knowing that too much would alter her in a way he would be powerless to change. He didn't want to make his mother a half-goddess – he simply wanted to save her life. Her eyes tracked him, stricken, but Loch just held her hand until he saw her take her first uninhibited breath, her lungs no longer rattling and a faint bloom brushing her cheeks. Seeing what he needed to, he leaned over to brush a kiss over each cheek and then her forehead.

"Be well, my heart. My mother, blood of my blood. My love for you transcends time and I will never regret having made this decision for you. I must go now – they'll find me here. Be safe – tell stories of me, as I live on through you," Loch whispered, and his mother's hands clenched his arms, tears seeping from her eyes as she shook her head.

"Too much. You've done too much. You should have let me go."

"Never too much. You've touched more in this lifetime, saved more people and done more good than I ever have. You've earned your right to stay and continue your good works. It is my gift to you, a son to his mother, one of the highest priestesses of the land and one of the most benevolent hearts I know. Continue your magick and plant a rose bush – think of me as they bloom," Loch said, then tilted his head to listen. Hearing the cries of the avengers on the wind, he pressed one last kiss to her cheek, delighted to see the light burning in her golden eyes – twins of his – once more.

Loch used his magick to whisk himself away, comforting himself with the fire that blazed in his mother's eyes and ignoring the pain he saw shadowed in their depths. What was done was done. He'd accept the consequences as a warrior – a high fae priest – did, and would take his mortal blow with grace.

Materializing outside the cave once again, he walked carefully inside, no longer using magick nor caring if the wards were tripped – alerting the Mireesi to his presence there. The safest thing he could do at his point would be to return the goddess's blood to its throne, at the very least ensuring it wouldn't fall into the wrong hands. Carrying such a treasure unprotected out in the world could lead to a mass revolution, worlds colliding, magicks of the darkest and most insidious powers rising up and seeping across the lands. At least here, in the moments before his certain death, he could return it safely.

Loch placed the bottle gently back on its pedestal, already knowing the avengers watched him from behind, but he didn't turn. Instead, he secured the bottle, making certain the ruby rose stopper was tightly secured and that the crystal bottle was once again surrounded by its magickal bonds. He took a moment to stare at the beauty held there, something no living fae had seen, before turning and dropping to his knees. Hanging his head, he awaited his final judgment, knowing that it would be instantaneous and irreversible. Sighing, he sent a quick spell of protection to his mother and awaited his end.

"Stand." A voice unbearably rich in beauty – both a choir singing and angels weeping – washed over him, making shivers rush through him and demanding an immediate response.

Loch stood, raising his eyes to see the Goddess Danu, having taken the form of a stunningly gorgeous woman, ripe with curves and lush in the prime of youth – an apple waiting to be plucked from the tree. Loch fought the immediate surge of lust that coursed through him, instead dropping his eyes from hers; he bowed deeply.

"Goddess," Loch said, his tone respectful, his eyes on the damp floor of the cave.

"Lochlain Laird, high priest of my people, what have you done?" Danu demanded, her voice causing twin spikes of lust and fear as Loch's mind raced, wondering how to play this out. The fact that he was still alive was unthinkable, and he wondered what that meant for him.

One thing Loch knew was that if he told her someone had

been given her blood, that person would be captured and quarantined, as it was still uncertain what magickal benefits a drop of goddess blood might unleash in a fae. Still certain his death was imminent, Loch raised his head and flashed a cocky grin at Danu.

"Just thought I'd see for myself what all the hype was about this cave. It's really quite interesting, all the artifacts in here." Loch glanced around, allowing insolence to infuse his manner before raking a hand through his hair and shrugging. "Certainly some lovely magicks."

Danu tilted her head, studying him, and the cave remained silent.

"You know, I've always liked you," Danu finally said, causing Loch's façade to crumble a bit as he caught her eyes in surprise. She walked slowly toward him, coming to stand but inches from his body, her power brushing over him, making every nerve ending he possessed go on high alert.

"Is that so?" Loch said, forcing himself to remain brash, though his mind whirled as he tried to resist the power of her. It threatened to sweep him under, rendering him defenseless.

"Yes. So strong," Danu said, stroking a hand up his arm, heat trailing in its wake, "Hot-headed, stubborn, and with a fierceness that very few warriors have. And yet, deep within lies a heart that is pure gold – one that makes choices for the good of others, often for the good of all." Danu continued to run her hand over his arm, stepping a breath closer as she looked up at him with eyes of amethyst, slanted at the corners, holding the secrets of the world in their depths.

"Only but to serve your highest wish, my goddess," Loch said, ignoring the invitation he saw in her eyes.

"I almost took you for a lover," Danu said, and Loch felt his stomach clench, his body responding against its own will to her words, as any man would in the face of such beauty and power. "But you are not for me," Danu said, patting his cheek gently before stepping back.

Loch, wisely, kept silent.

Danu paced a few steps, her arms tucked behind her as she considered her options, the Mireesi standing steely behind her, their eyes never leaving Loch.

"Why did you take my blood?" Danu asked, meeting his eyes directly. Loch felt the force of her pressing into his mind, seeking the answers. Shielding against her with all his magick and mental acuity – and unsure whether it would be enough – Loch once again lied in the face of the highest power in all the worlds.

"I just wanted to see what powers it held," Loch said, shrugging.

"And? Did you find what you sought?" Danu asked, cocking an eyebrow at him as she planted a hand on her hip.

"Aye, I did at that. Very powerful magick, my goddess." Loch dared to smile cheekily at her, not caring so much anymore, as his death was certain now.

"And you will accept the consequences of your actions – no matter what they may be – as you're guilty of one of the highest crimes a Danula can commit?" Danu asked, her eyes never leaving his.

"Aye, my goddess. I accept my death with apologies for my actions," Loch said.

"You will not tell me what you stole my blood for?" Danu asked for the second time, her power probing his mind, while Loch fought to keep her out and protect his mother.

"I told you – curiosity. As you said yourself, I'm stubborn. It was very difficult for me not to know the secrets this cave held. Now I do, but to my own detriment. I shall serve as a lesson for others," Loch said and waited once more for her to order his demise. He couldn't understand why she was dallying with him, as every fae knew that entering this cave was certain death.

"Your words are only that – words," Danu said, a smile briefly flitting across her face before she raised her exquisite chin high, her arms lifting above her head as she began to deliver her orders. "However, in this case, your power is yet needed in this world. You've a service to perform, and you shall do so, before I render my final decision on your continued existence in this realm. In lieu of instant mortality for having broken the most sacred of magicks to enter my sacred realm, for daring to touch and use my most enchanted of blood, I am commanding you, Lochlain, to join Na Cosantoir and to protect the Seeker, the third in this quest, and to ensure no harm comes to her until she finds the treasure. You will be allowed to live for the time being, until the bounds of the quest are met and the treasure is secured. At that point, I will decide upon your fate."

Surprise seized Loch as he realized the goddess was sparing his life – followed immediately by wrath.

"You want me to follow some girl around to make sure she can find a treasure? But that is a mere soldier's job," Loch scoffed – then caught himself. Best not to be too arrogant. More time in this world would allow him to ensure that his mother was healthy and thriving.

"Na Cosantoir is a great honor among our people, Lochlain. For generations Danula have sought this role to ensure the protection of our people," Danu said, sounding as miffed as a goddess could.

"For those with little power, yes, I can see the appeal of

such a role," Loch quickly amended. "However, my talents are better served in other areas."

Danu drew herself up and the temperature of the room dropped as her temper ratcheted up.

"This is not a negotiation. You will do as I say or your life is null and void," Danu said, crystals freezing on her breath and cracking in mid-air as her anger washed over Loch, causing ice to slick across his skin.

"Yes, my goddess. My deepest apologies. I will ensure that this... Seeker... finds her way to the treasure," Loch bit out, hating that he was being cursed with such a mundane task, far beneath his prowess as a high priest.

"You do so. Or your life is mine."

In a cloud of ice crystals and magicks, the goddess disappeared, leaving Loch blinded as he stood gasping in surprise at the turn of events. When he finally dared to open his eyes, he grimaced.

Before him stood a small village in the country, and more importantly, the arts and crafts store which he sensed held the Seeker he was to protect. Seeing several Star Wars posters, stacks of comics on tables in the window, and piles of notebooks, stationery, markers, knick-knacks, toys, and bits and bobs of lace, Loch shook his head in disbelief. This was his Seeker's shop?

Groaning, he settled in to wait.

CHAPTER 3

Gwenith Donovan turned the pages of the latest Marvel comic, her eyes tracing every illustration with awe as she cheerfully followed the storyline – even though she was getting a little tired of the sexualizing of the female lead.

"I mean…come on. Does every woman in comics need to have a twenty-inch waist and boobs out to here?" Gwen scoffed to the cat sunning itself lazily in the window. "Don't they know women can be badass warriors that come in all shapes and sizes?"

Macgregor, her oversized tabby cat, slitted an eye open at her words. Seeing no promise of food, he stretched and went back to sleep.

"Yeah, yeah, I know. Sex sells." Gwen waved a hand at the cat and went back to finishing the comic book, comfortable in her own skin and what she deemed a complete lack of sex appeal. She always envisioned herself kind of like a potato, lumpy and curvy and round. So very, very round. With a mass of curling red hair, which she pulled into a loose knot on her head most days, guileless blue eyes, and porcelain skin that betrayed her every emotion with the slightest flush, Gwen had stopped worrying whether she was sexy ages ago. It was much easier to maintain a cheerful life and live in her dreams than it was to repeatedly put herself out there and be found lacking by the men of her tiny village.

"Still a good story. I'd give it seven out of ten," Gwen decided. She slipped the comic back into a clear plastic envelope to protect its pages, and added it to her file folder holding this year's editions of the series. She was always optimistic about the value of comics, proclaiming far and wide to all who would listen that someday she could sell them for thousands. Well, maybe hundreds, she thought with a snort, but at least it kept people from judging her collection too harshly.

"Well, Mac, what's on the agenda for today? Should we lock up soon? It's a wee bit slow, though we're finally getting some of that sunshine they've been promising us," Gwen said, puttering around her shop and straightening this and that, humming the opening bars to Celine Dion's "My Heart Will Go On."

Perpetually cheerful, Gwen always had an optimistic viewpoint. Frankly, she couldn't ask for much more – she loved her shop, loved her family, and even loved the tiny village she called home. There was nothing she wanted for; her needs were met and she was able to run a store surrounded by the things she loved every day.

Some would point out that romance was missing, but Gwen had given up on that aspect of her life ages ago. Less to fuss about, she thought. And once she took sex out of the equation – not that she knew anything about it – she'd been able to have many great male friends in her life. Aye, her needs were met and she'd be hard pressed to complain about anything at all. For the most part, it seemed that sex and romance caused nothing but heartache and stress, and she had patted more than one friend's back as they'd struggled their way through break-ups. Life would be so much easier if people stopped worrying so much about sex, Gwen thought, eyeing a stand of thank-you cards that needed to be rearranged. Within fifteen minutes or so, Gwen had sorted out her display of cards, rotating in new inventory, and stepped back to admire her work. With a glance at the clock, she decided it was time to call it quits for the day.

Mondays were generally slow in the village, and even more so with a novelty shop. She should probably just close the store on the slow days, but Gwen so enjoyed being surrounded by the things she loved that she couldn't quite bring herself to stay away. What else was she to do anyway? She already spent her spare time having a pint with friends or helping out a neighbor in a bind, watching their kids – no reason not to show up for an honest day's work.

But slipping out early also had its benefits – namely, her gran wouldn't question where she was and she could work on experimenting with a little secret she'd discovered. Gwen clutched her hands to her chest and almost squealed in delight, except it would have startled Macgregor. She couldn't even bring herself to say the words out loud, lest someone overhear it – lest it be taken away from her.

But... she just might – Gwen bit back a giggle at the thought – she just might actually have a magickal power. Like a real-life comic book heroine! She paused and put her hand in the air – holding it up like Katniss in The Hunger Games and standing proudly. Oh yes, yes indeed, Gwen thought; she could get on board with this magickal power thing.

"Time to practice," Gwen said, going to the back of the shop and unlatching the small kitty door – but a mere hole with a door and a latch – that would allow Macgregor to wander up to her flat above the shop. Though she'd lived there for a few years now, happily puttering about in her little space, Gwen still checked on or had dinner with her Gran nearly every night after work. Family was family, and she sure did love her small family of Gran and her dog, Chauncy.

She'd be sure to stop and bring Gran some of the cordial she fancied, Gwen decided, feeling a smidgen of guilt as she turned off the lights and locked up the extra cash from the till. It was truly the first secret she'd kept from Gran, and she wasn't happy about doing it. However, until she wrapped her head around what she'd discovered, it was best that she remain silent.

Plus, she wasn't willing to share quite yet. For the first time in her very sheltered life, Gwen was anything but ordinary.

And that was certainly worth holding onto for a little bit longer.

CHAPTER 4

*L*och straightened from where he'd leaned against the wall of a chemist across the street from his Seeker's shop. 'This & That' was the name lettered in bright gold on the window, and Loch scoffed. How was a body supposed to know what was sold there if the name of the shop wasn't clear? This & That could be anything – at least with a supermarket or a chemist, a person would know what was inside.

People veered around Loch, unable to see him due to a cloaking spell he'd used but sensing something was in their path anyway. Irritation built in him as he waited for the Seeker to emerge. Not used to waiting, Loch almost bounded across the street and pulled her out, but forced himself to hang back and watch. Best not to blow his cover, he thought, until he knew the lay of the land better, and knew what exactly he was dealing with.

Which wasn't a very bright-minded individual, Loch all but snorted. This & That. What a name.

Loch watched as the door finally opened, something he'd

expected moments ago when he'd seen the lights switch off. Restraint was not one of his stronger traits, but he forced himself not to react when he saw the woman step out of her shop and look around once before turning to lock the door.

Why did she dress like she hated her body? Loch wondered. The women in his fae village prided themselves on wearing beautifully rendered clothing, cloaking themselves in silks and linens and acres of sparkling jewelry – the fae did love sparkly things. It would be considered an affront to the beauty of what they were to dress as if they disliked their shape.

And, oh, was this woman shapely, Loch thought – at least from what he could ascertain from the baggy clothes she wore. Loose cargo pants were tucked into wellington boots and stretched across a curvy bum as she bent to latch the door, and when she turned, an oversized cream woolen cardigan hung open nearly to her knees, with a loose t-shirt proclaiming "The force is strong with this one" belying the ample breasts hidden beneath. Red hair – siren red, Loch thought, tucked so tightly on her head that he itched to pull the pins out and see it tumble down. What looked to be brilliant blue eyes completed the bedraggled look.

Except for that mouth, Loch thought, unable to draw his gaze away from her cupid's bow of a mouth, like an unplucked rose, plump and inviting against the porcelain of her skin. It was a mouth that was meant to be tasted, kissed until swollen, and then tasted once more. When a tug of lust tightened his chest, Loch was surprised at himself. Used to being highly sought-after in his world, he'd had more than his fair share of beautiful lovers – from timid and blushing to experienced courtesans. There was nothing commanding about this woman's presence – if anything, it was as though she wished to blend into the crowd.

It wasn't often that someone, especially a human, perplexed him. Loch didn't like it. He was used to getting a quick read on a person and understanding a situation immediately. His body's response to this woman was anything but expected. Had Danu charmed him in some way so that he would be drawn to this Seeker?

Lost in his thoughts, he almost missed seeing when the Seeker slipped abruptly into an alley, disappearing quickly from the hustle and bustle of the little village's main street. Intrigued, Loch crossed the street and made his way down the alley. Though he couldn't see her, it was as if he could track her in his mind's eye. This was a well-known gift the Protectors were given, often spoken about in the fae world, and something he'd yet to experience. But now? He seemed to be almost mated to this woman, for he could follow her as though she'd given him explicit directions well in advance.

To the water they went, both Seeker and Protector carefully making their way from the village, following a narrow, winding path that eventually fed out to a small sheltered inlet, one not visible from the village's main wharf. Loch had to wonder why she came to this place – though it certainly was beautiful.

It only took moments before Loch began to curse.

CHAPTER 5

"*N*ow, let's see if I've figured this out," Gwen murmured, coming to a stop just short of the water's edge. This little beach was a favorite of hers, known only to the locals, and not much longer than the width of her shop. Surrounded on all sides by land that rose far above her head, she had total privacy unless a boat motored past. If someone came down the path, she'd hear them pushing through the bushes long before they would see her.

Gwen emptied her brain and worked on what she'd been reading about the use of magickal powers – essentially a mix of visualizing and feeling the outcome of what her wishes were. And her wish was to turn the water gently lapping over the pebbles at her feet into ice.

Oh, but she'd been exhilarated the first time it had happened. She'd almost dropped the glass she'd been holding, she'd been so shocked, catching it an instant before it slipped completely from her hand. It had been one of those unseasonably warm spring days – highly unusual for Ireland – and she'd been sweating in her shop. Having taken off her cardigan, she'd looked at her water and said something along the lines of 'if this was the States I'd have an ice machine for my drinks.' Knowing the Americans' love of ice, the thought had just popped up in her head.

What she hadn't expected was for ice to pop up in her drink as well.

It was one of those quintessential life-changing moments she read about in novels, where nothing would ever be the same again, Gwen thought. She'd screeched, sending Macgregor skidding through the shop, then picked the fat tabby up to dance around in delight before setting him down to try to create ice once more.

She wasn't exactly proud of how long it had taken her to hone the ability, and after a few mishaps and one regrettable burst pipe, she'd learned to take the magick outside and practice in private.

It still thrilled her, every time, when water solidified before her eyes as it did now. Where once the water had gently caressed the pebbles at her feet, now a thin layer of ice ensconced them, clear and smooth, looking for all the world like glass. Gwen clapped her hands in delight, looking down at the beauty of what she'd created.

She had done this, Gwen thought, as she clasped her hands to her chest and twirled in delight. She, Gwen Donovan, had magickal powers like the warrior women in her comic books! Now, if only she could figure out the best use of her powers.

When her eyes collided with another's, Gwen squeaked. It was the only sound she could make as a man, seeming to glow with a silver hue, stepped silently from the bushes from where he'd been watching her. His eyes darted left and right, tracking her every move, and Gwen immediately realized he was danger with a capital D.

"Um, hello, then. I didn't see you there," Gwen said, smiling and deciding to put on a cheerful unconcerned air, though her hand groped for the small knife she'd tucked in her pocket.

The man said nothing, but he didn't need to. His smile said it all.

Gwen shrieked, pulling the knife from her pocket as he lunged for her, but already knew she wasn't fast enough. She was going to fail, through her own fault, like the person who runs upstairs in a scary movie instead of out the front door. She'd cornered herself and hadn't even had her protection accessible. It was her own damn fault if she died today, Gwen thought, then gasped when the man seemed to stop in mid-step, his eyes widening and his mouth open on a silent scream.

Shocked, Gwen looked down to where an iron spike protruded from the man's chest, silvery liquid seeping from the edges of the wound. In seconds, the man dissolved into a silver puddle of liquid at her feet, the now-thawed water swallowing the blood. *Was* it blood? Gwen dazedly wondered as she drew her gaze from the dwindling puddle across a pair of black-as-night boots, to well-muscled legs clad in the blackest of leather, up further past a muscled chest, to shoulders that nearly doubled the width of hers, and finally to a sharply angled face glaring at her in disgust.

Oh, he's the superhero, Gwen thought, the breath all but leaving her body as she met golden eyes – almost tawny like a tiger's – and dark hair that her fingers itched to touch. A real-life superhero and he was here to save her.

"Thank you," Gwen said, swallowing against a dry throat

and smiling up at the glowering stranger. "I'm not entirely sure what that was about, but as I'm certain he meant to cause me harm, I'm indebted to you for your help. It is much appreciated." She wondered briefly if she should curtsy, but it seemed overkill.

"You're indebted? You have no idea what you owe me. You stupid twit, you could've endangered our very existence! What are you doing running around practicing your magick out in the open? Unprotected? You might as well be a sitting duck for the Domnua! Are you out of your damn mind? Of course they give me the senseless one," the superhero muttered, beginning to pace as he shot her lightning bolts from under dark brows.

Did he just call her senseless? Gwen felt her Irish ratchet up a bit at his words.

"Excuse me – you don't even know me, so you can't yet decide if I am senseless or not. But I'll be telling you that I don't know what a Domnua is and I'm certain I wasn't doing anything to draw attention to myself. So you can just calm down with this whole tough guy act, buddy," Gwen snapped, her hands at her hips as she glared at him.

"Lochlain – Loch, that is," the man said. Distracted by his anger, he all but pulled his hair out as he ran his hands through it. What was he going to do with this twit of a girl? "This & That? What kind of name is that for a store? That doesn't show much sense. Much like your practicing magick in the open. I forbid you from doing so again, unless you'd like to see yourself made non-existent."

"It's a damn good name for a store that carries everything," Gwen practically shouted at Loch. How dare he insult her store – her favorite thing in the world? "And I'll be practicing magick as much as I damn well please, you overbearing bully!" With that, Gwen gathered all the still-untested power from deep within her and blasted him with a fury of ice. She gasped as it coated him from head to foot, freezing him in place, ice crystals forming on his eyebrows. Shocked, overwhelmed, and oddly giddy, Gwen half-screeched and half-laughed as she tore around the frozen superhero and ran up the hill, leaving him behind her to sort himself out.

As she was certain he would – men like that always did. Her heart thumping in her chest, Gwen didn't stop until she was barricaded in her apartment where she could gleefully relive every detail of her first superhero encounter.

Her life was turning out to be far more exciting than she'd ever anticipated.

CHAPTER 6

*W*as that someone laughing? Loch wiped water from his face and looked around, glaring, for the offender: one of his brethren, a tall wiry man with a shock of red hair and a grey leather jacket, almost falling down the side of the cliff as his body shook with laughter.

"Aye, mate, I'm glad I was here to see that." The man wiped tears from his eyes and Loch felt his lips draw up in a snarl.

"And why exactly are you here?" Loch asked the fae, his tone even, though he was silently thinking of all the ways he could murder the man.

"Right, right, about that – the name's Seamus," the red-haired fae said, bouncing down the side of the hill and landing easily on his feet before holding out a hand. "Myself and my better half are here to assist you on your quest."

Loch eyed the hand in front of him with disdain, but his mother's manners won out and he clasped it quickly before dropping it.

"Lochlain."

"Aye, sure and I'm knowing who you are. 'Tis a right pleasure to be meeting yourself, it is." Seamus beamed at him. "I've heard many a tale of the great magicks you can wield and your prowess on a battlefield. I was wondering if the next Protector would be more powerful. It seems to me as though the Domnua are ratcheting things up – putting on the pressure, so to speak. Your powers will be right valuable, that's the truth of it."

"I'm not using my powers on this silly quest. It's beneath me is what it is, nothing but a punishment," Loch said through gritted teeth, his hands clenching at his sides as he thought about what the goddess was forcing him into. He'd prefer death at this point than to have to deal with the flighty, giggly, irascible... decadent, begging to be unbuttoned... Loch shook his head and focused back on hating his mission instead of the unexpected charms of Miss Gwenith. It wouldn't do for him to get distracted anyway, seeing as how it would only get her or anyone else around them killed if he did.

"Sure and I can see how this would seem to be a bit outside your usual realm, but you can't really argue that saving the entire Danula as well as the human race by keeping the Domnua banished to the underworld is a task befitting just anyone, can you?" Seamus asked, rocking back on his heels and crossing his arms over his chest, a cheeky grin on his face. "I'd say it's an honor."

"I didn't ask what you'd say." Loch glowered at him, and then ran a quick spell to dry himself from the remnants of the ice storm Gwen had unleashed upon him. Someone was going to have to set the chit straight, and it looked like it was going to be him. Cursing once again, he turned to go.

"Hey, where are you going?"

"It appears I need to teach this Seeker a few lessons," Loch growled, then almost rolled his eyes when Seamus fell into step next to him, like a puppy following a bigger dog and wanting to play.

"Might I suggest an attitude change?" Seamus said, and Loch drew to a stop so quickly that Seamus was a few steps ahead before he realized Loch was no longer walking.

"I'm sorry, but I'm certain I must have misheard you," Loch said, his tone deadly, his eyes flashing a warning at Seamus.

"I said, might I suggest an attitude change? This whole tough guy thing is great for battle but you're going to end up scaring Gwen, not to mention being a bitch to work with on this quest. It'd be easier for everyone if you just calmed down a bit and worked at being a team player – we're all in this together, after all," Seamus said, his eyes never leaving Loch's. He barely flinched when Loch lifted him from the ground with one hand gripped tightly around Seamus' neck.

"You don't speak to me like that," Loch said, enunciating each word carefully so the simpleton would understand how grievously he'd overstepped his boundaries.

"And you don't get to ruin the fate of our world for the sake of your own damn ego," Seamus said, a faint flush beginning to tinge his cheeks.

Loch knew the man was struggling to breathe. Cursing, he put Seamus on his feet and turned to stare out across the water, his look impenetrable, much like the smooth surface of the water. But beneath the calm veneer, rage boiled.

Damn it, but the man was right. And there was nothing Loch hated more than admitting that someone else was right.

"Fine," Loch said, turning to Seamus, who stood studying him. "I'll work on my delivery. Is that better?"

"You're still scary as shite, but yeah, it's a mite less frightening if you tone it down a bit. Now, we'd best go find my lovely woman so we can spend a little time debriefing you on what's happened before you go off and scare the piss out of Gwen again."

"She didn't seem all that scared of me," Loch said, as he and Seamus climbed the hill.

"That's what I like about her – much like me own Bianca. I love a lass with spirit," Seamus said, his voice cheerful again. Loch had to admire that the man had taken his little display of temper in stride and hadn't batted an eye at being almost choked to death. Perhaps he would be a good asset on the journey.

"Women are nothing but trouble," Loch bit out.

"The best kind of trouble, my friend, only the best kind."

CHAPTER 7

*G*wen bounced around the room, sending Macgregor running, as she clapped her hands in front of her face, trying to hold back the hysterical giggles that threatened to overtake her.

"Oh but Macgregor – if only you'd seen him!" Gwen patted her cheeks, which she could feel were afire with excitement. "He was like every superhero I've ever read about. Or even more than that – I swear, in a comic book we wouldn't even be sure if he was the good guy or the bad guy. Had he come up to me first instead of the silver one, well, shoot, I would have thought he was the bad guy."

Gwen twirled around the room, almost manic with delight. Not only did she have magickal powers, but she'd met others with powers as well. Granted, one of them had tried to kill her, but that was just a minor detail. Everyone knew that wielding power came with some downsides.

"With great power comes great responsibility," Gwen intoned, quoting Spiderman to Macgregor, who just rolled onto his back to look up at her.

"I'm telling you, Mac, he was gorgeous with a capital G. The kind of man women dream of," Gwen said. Mac rolled again, cocking his head as if he were actually listening.

Gwen pulled off her cardigan and danced her way across the living room – nothing more than a small one-bedroom apartment. And that was using the word 'bedroom' loosely, Gwen thought as she tossed the cardigan on her double bed, which took up almost the entirety of the room. A single bed would have made more sense, but she loved being able to stretch out and snuggle into her pillows. There was nothing she loved more than curling up on a rainy evening with a favorite book. No, her bedroom was a sanctuary for her, and she'd been right to buy the double bed.

Gwen hummed as she hung her cardigan back up in the teeny closet in the corner of the room, and quickly changed from her Star Wars t-shirt into a vintage long-sleeved Wonder Woman one. Singing, she bustled around her apartment with Macgregor two steps behind her, waiting for his nightly snack.

"Oh, Mac, I swear this has just been the best day. I all but swooned when I saw Loch. I mean, he saved my life and he's handsome as sin? It's hard not to feel my heart go aflutter at that." Gwen laughed at herself. "But honestly, guys like him never look twice at girls like me. And that's just fine, isn't it? Because you and I both know he is nothing but trouble. And I do mean trooouble."

Macgregor meowed at her as if he agreed, and Gwen chuckled, stepping to her tiny kitchenette and pulling out a tin of his favorite wet food. As he wound himself between her legs, desperate for his snack, Gwen chattered on about her amazing experience with Loch and how she'd even used her power in a way she hadn't known was possible.

She paused. He had called her stupid, which was annoying – and he'd insulted her shop. If she ever met him again, she was certain he would think twice about repeating the same mistake. Gwen laughed, remembering the surprise on his face when she'd coated him in ice. It had been nothing but an instinctive response – but he'd deserved it, the silly man. Someone had to teach men like that a lesson. It was best he learned that he couldn't just say whatever he wanted, whenever he wanted.

"I'm telling you, Mac, this is a real-life comic book. I'd say fairy-tale, but there's no romance to be found here." Gwen chuckled once more. It was oddly comforting knowing that she wouldn't have a man like Loch pursuing her. Not only was she confident that he didn't go for women like her, but she was well aware that she wouldn't know the first thing to do if a man like that did turn an eye on her.

"It sure is fun to look though," Gwen said, then blew Mac a kiss as she locked up to go to dinner at her gran's. There was nothing wrong with looking – or even appreciating a finely built man – so long as she didn't expect anything from it.

Gwen had learned long ago that expectations were the death of dreams.

And she was never going to stop dreaming.

CHAPTER 8

The little village hummed with energy and light, even on a Monday, and it was part of the reason that Gwen found it so hard to leave this place. And what for? She had all she needed, right in this little town, and nights like this showcased why it was such a great place to live.

She waved at people as she wandered up the street, her head in the clouds, her smile automatic for those who called to her by name.

Pausing at the small bookstore, she poked her head in.

"Anything new, Agnes?" Gwen called.

"Shipment's in tomorrow, Gwennie. I'll be letting you know if I've got anything good for you." Agnes waved from the back, never lowering the book she held in front of her face.

"Thanks, Love," Gwen called back, and decided to detour to the bakery and see if they had any of the baguettes her gran so loved to serve. In no time at all, Gwen was out of the shop and on her way. Whistling, her arms full of bread and the cookies she couldn't bring herself to resist, Gwen paused at the top of the hill to turn and admire her village. The sun was just setting, its rays casting a golden balm across the houses and shops nestled into the hillside on the water; lights twinkled out of homes where mothers yelled at children to wash up before dinner, and the first strains of a music session tinkled out from the open door of a pub.

Yes, it was a good place to live. City life wasn't for her; she'd learned that fairly quickly after she'd tried a year at uni in Dublin. The hustle and bustle, the sharp edges of people's attitudes, the lack of open green space – it had been enough to set Gwen on edge. And she wasn't someone who liked to be on edge. When she'd found herself having yet another argument with her flatmate, she'd thrown in the towel and come home. Gwen hated fighting about as much as she hated the concrete jungle of Dublin. It was only when she'd returned back to the village and seen the little shop for sale that she knew what she wanted to do with her life.

And the rest, as they say, is history.

Or so she'd thought. Gwen smiled and continued up the hill toward her gran's house, tucked away at the end of a street. Wasn't that always the way of things, then? As soon as you thought you had things figured out, life threw you a plot twist, Gwen thought, cheerful as ever. It wasn't that she didn't like her life… but perhaps it had grown a wee bit stagnant. That's why this new development was so delightful. It was like her life was already a delicious scone, and finding out she had magickal powers was akin to adding cinnamon sugar butter to the top of it.

Satisfied with her metaphor, Gwen continued to her gran's house, her head in the clouds, unaware of the odd stillness that had pervaded the street.

Had she been more alert, she would have noticed the three

men leaning against a wall of the alley, their eyes tracking her every move. Instead, she breezed right past, contemplating new ways to use her magick, when the hair at the back of her neck stood up. Ducking instinctively, Gwen gaped at the knife sticking out of the wall where her head had just been.

The bakery bag dropped from her arms as she whirled to find three of the silvery men coming at her fast. Not knowing where to look or what to do, Gwen gasped as one landed a hard left to her stomach. Forcing herself not to recoil – she knew that doing so would mean death – Gwen sucked in air as she staggered a step back, her arms coming in front of her.

"I'd suggest you back off. I know tae kwon do," Gwen said, lying through her teeth. The silver men circled, saying nothing, their eyes following her every movement. When one darted at her, Gwen did the only thing she could think of.

She iced him.

Gwen squeaked as he shattered into thousands of silver shards. It was like watching a rock come sailing through a glass window and disintegrating before her eyes. Barely having time to register what had just happened, she squeaked again as a blur of movement – black leather movement this time – quickly made silver puddles of the other two men.

"Uh, you're back," Gwen said. Her heart hitched a bit as she trailed her eyes up all that leather to the furious face of Loch glaring down at her.

"Aye, against my will, I'm back," Loch said.

"Well, excuse me, but I don't know who you are or what you want. Nobody is forcing you to be here. You can just go on your merry way," Gwen said, surprising herself with how rude she was being to him. Hadn't the man just saved her? But it seemed as though being around him made her want to spit nails – which was about as far away from Gwen's typical demeanor as she could get.

Schooling her face into a pleasant smile, she channeled her gran's company manners. "I'm sorry. That was rude of me. Thank you very much for your assistance. I wish you luck on your journey, wherever that may take you. I'm certain I can handle any of..." Gwen waved her hand at the last dredges of silver liquid slipping into the earth. "Whatever this is."

Loch stepped close, his nearness forcing her to take one step back, then two, until her back was pressed to the wall where the knife was still embedded. He reached over her shoulder and easily slipped the knife from the wood, wiping it absently on his leathers before slipping it in his waistband. Gwen tried not to look when he lifted his shirt, but she was human, wasn't she? And the glimpse of tanned muscular abs would have made any woman sigh.

"Eyes up here," Loch said.

Gwen started, embarrassed to have been caught staring. The smirk on his face was enough to get her temper rising.

"Then don't be swaggering in here and flashing me all that skin. A girl can look, you know," she sputtered.

Loch's face became even more unreadable, if such a thing was possible.

"I don't swagger."

"You most certainly do swagger. I know a swagger when I see one – and you swagger. Your overbearing king-of-the-world act is unnecessary," Gwen bit out, still pressed against the wall, her body but mere inches from his. Was it him radiating all that warmth? Or perhaps it was just the adrenaline coursing through her from the recent attack of those... things.

"Seamus warned me about this," Loch sighed, raking a hand through his hair.

"Seamus is…?"

"Danula, like myself. Good fae. And what you just killed there was a Domnua. The bad fae, if you will," Loch said, shaking his head at her.

A rushing sound seemed to fill Gwen's ears, drowning out the rest of what he said. All she heard was the word 'fae.' As in fairies. The fae were real? Her mind flashed to her gran's stories about how she had grown up. Nothing but nonsense, Gwen had always thought, but had contented herself with enjoying the stories. 'Gwen who dances with fairies.' It had a nonsensical ring to it, and she'd never pressed her gran too much on stories of her real parents. Why would she? It was obviously a difficult thing for Gran to talk about, and the last thing Gwen ever wanted to do was to hurt those she loved.

But now? This – well, this was too much. It was time to have a talk with Gran about the 'dancing with fairies' story.

She surprised even herself when she pushed Loch away – hard enough to have him take a half-step back – before slipping under his arm.

"I have to go."

"Gwen, we need to talk."

"I'm not ready to talk to you right now," Gwen said, her nose in the air. Then she stopped short – he was suddenly in front of her, blocking her movement, but a whisper of air, he'd moved so fast.

"You don't have a say in the matter," Loch said.

Gwen raised a finger, pointing it right at his face – as rude as she'd ever been. "I do have a say in the matter. You don't own me, you don't control me, and you don't get to tell me what to do. Now get the hell out of my way. I'll talk to you when I'm good and ready to talk to you," she hissed, alarmed at herself. Who was this woman? Not a single person who knew her had ever heard her speak like this – not even her old flatmate in Dublin.

"That's fine, Gwen who dances with fairies," Loch said, a dangerous smile slipping over his face at her enraged expression, "Let me know when you're ready to dance."

Gwen gaped at him as he strolled away as if he had not a care in the world.

"Aye, that's a swagger," Gwen called after him.

His laugh, raspy enough to sound unused, flitted back to her on the wind – then he was gone, leaving a thousand questions in his wake.

CHAPTER 9

*G*wen grabbed the bag of bread – miraculously still intact – and raced the rest of the way up the street. She burst through the front door of her gran's house, her chest heaving as she struggled for air.

"Why, whatever is the rush, my dear? You certainly came in all in a tizzy," Gran said, poking her head out from the kitchen at the back of the little house. A row house, attached to others on either side, the cozy home was set up like a square with a sitting room and a dining room in front, the kitchen in back, and three small bedrooms and one bath upstairs. Gwen supposed it wasn't anything grand, but it had always been home to her and one of her favorite places in the world. She had fond memories of growing up dancing down the streets with the children next door and playing games in the small garden out back.

"Gwen who dances with fairies. That's a true story, isn't it? Not just a fairytale?" Gwen asked. Her heart seemed to stop beating in her chest as a moment of silence stretched between them.

Gran said nothing for a moment, but the truth was in her eyes.

Gwen held up a hand, stopping any words that might come out. "I can see it's the truth," she said, trying to wrap her head around the story.

"Oh, Gwen, I'm so sorry." Her pint-sized Gran moved to stand in front of her, her tiny frame trembling with angst as she twisted the dishtowel between her fingers. "I should have told you – but how could I? Even I know it sounds crazy. And I wanted to keep you so badly – I loved you so much."

Suddenly realizing that her gran was terrified she would be upset, Gwen snapped out of her thoughts.

"Are you kidding me? This is amazing!" Gwen swept her gran into a jig and danced her down the hallway, the older woman still light on her feet after all these years, and laughed. "Seriously, don't you know how cool this is? I've always thought I was a bit boring, but I'm not at all! I have magick!"

Gran laughed as Gwen released her, but Gwen caught the shimmer of tears in her eyes.

"Don't cry, please don't. I'm not mad at you. I always figured there was more to the story about my parents, but since it seemed like such a painful subject to you, I just tucked it away. It wouldn't and still doesn't change what is – my love for you. You're my family and that's that," Gwen said. She hugged her gran as tears ran in rivulets down the old woman's still-pretty face.

"Oh, I've been so worried about this day. I should have known, I really should have known better. You have such a lightness in you – such a beautiful gift of optimism and seeing the best in everyone and every situation. I should have known you wouldn't begrudge me this. But I was so worried

I would lose you or you'd hate me." Gran went back to the stove and stood there for a beat, taking a deep breath before filling the kettle with water. A time-honored tradition, making tea, in good times and bad, and the comfort of the routine seemed to calm Gran.

"I know you love me. You don't have a mean bone in your body. There's no way you would have tried to hide this from me unless you were worried it would hurt me. I know you, Gran. Trust me when I say this – I don't feel betrayed. It's just so exciting to think about all the fae legends and things I don't know about. I mean, I've read about some of this stuff, but I have so much to learn," Gwen said, dropping into a chair as the endless possibilities washed over her.

"Aye, fairies are very real, my child," Gran said, smiling gently as she brought the tea to the table, arranging the cups just so and allowing the pot of tea to steep as she dropped into the chair across from Gwen.

"So, am I a fairy then? I mean... I guess I am, right? What can you tell me?" Gwen asked, reaching into the bag for the cookies. Now was a time for cookies if ever there was one.

"Aye, you're fae. Or part-fae. I'm not entirely sure on the details of that," Gran admitted, taking a cookie and biting into it. Gwen waited while the sugar did its work, then, when her gran looked a bit less tense, gestured for her to go on. "Well, as you know, I always told you the story of you dancing with fairies – that part was true."

"I danced with fairies?" Gwen all but bounced in her seat at the thought.

"You did. I always wondered how I stumbled on you that day – it was as though I'd stepped through a wall into a new world," Gran mused, her eyes going a bit dreamy as she thought back.

"What were you doing?" Gwen asked, taking another cookie from the plate. Calories be damned – she needed her energy.

"I'd gone for a drive that day and then a hike. I'm not sure what drew me down the coast, but I felt compelled to go. Oh, I'd been having one of my days – where I was feeling melancholy, missing Henry, and I suppose just out of sorts with life. You know I'm not one to fuss much over things, but everyone has their days."

Gwen reached out to squeeze Gran's hand. Henry had been her husband; he'd been lost in a fishing accident when a storm had rolled in and he'd hit his head, being tossed overboard. They'd never had children, so Gran had been on her own since then. Though Gwen knew that part of the story, she'd always assumed she was an orphan, and that perhaps she was just destined to be with Gran to keep her from being lonely. Since she'd had a happy childhood and loved her life, Gwen had never delved too deeply into the question of her parents. It hadn't mattered – family was family.

"Anyway, I was fussing a bit and went for a drive down the coast, and ended up parking by some abandoned hills that were quite overgrown. I can't quite remember ever having a yen to explore them before, but something drew me to them that day. At the time I thought perhaps I just needed a good walk to work off the head of mad I had going on. Now I know it was to find you."

"I wonder if I should go back to those hills. Was it a fae village?"

"It was… like nothing I've ever really seen before. As I said, it was like I'd stepped through a veil into another world

– perhaps another time. One second I was hiking up the hill, huffing out my mad, and the next I'd stepped into a field decorated for a party. I realize now it was a going-away party for you."

"Oh… oh, just wow," Gwen said, holding her hand to her heart. Why was this affecting her so?

"There were poles wound in flowers – almost like those maypoles, you know? And strands of streamers, flowers, and crystals – just hanging in the air, not attached to anything. Everything was alight and shimmering. And the fae... oh, they were such beautiful people – much like yourself – and they glimmered and shone as they danced and danced."

Gwen brushed off her gran's compliment. After all, she'd told Gwen all her life that she was beautiful. Seeing as how none of the men in the village seemed to second that sentiment, Gwen chalked it up to Gran's love for her clouding her judgment.

"And in the middle, there you were. Oh, but not even a year old, just toddling for the first time, your steps uncertain, yet you laughed and laughed. You were this beautiful chubby baby that was all joy. All around you the fae laughed and smiled back, singing their magickal songs. I couldn't not walk forward. It was as though I was being pulled to you – I had to go pick you up. I don't know, perhaps compelled is the word? I wasn't even scared or anything, though I certainly should have been. I just walked right into the middle of the circle and scooped you up – my dancing and laughing Gwen – and hugged you so tightly."

"What happened then?" Gwen could barely breathe. She'd heard this story, but never through the lens of it being real. All of a sudden, every detail mattered.

"Everything disappeared. It was like a light switch had

been flipped and all the flowers and dancing fae just…" Gran snapped her fingers. "…disappeared. It was the craziest thing. And there I was, in the middle of the hills holding a toddler I knew nothing about. And you know what you did?"

"I do, but tell me anyway," Gwen said, smiling at her gran.

"You turned and put your chubby little hands on my face and kissed me. You were nothing but pure joy, and you've been nothing but joy my whole life. A gift is what you are, my beautiful Gwen," Gran said, her heart in her eyes.

"I think you're the gift, Gran. You've been the best thing for me – both mother and father – letting me be me. I have had an interesting, lively, and beautiful upbringing. I couldn't have asked for more," Gwen said, smiling at her gran over her cup of tea.

"You wouldn't have, you know. You wouldn't have asked for more. You never do. You've always been happy with your lot in life and whenever something bad has happened, you've flipped it in your mind until it's good. It's a blessing you've been to me, my Gwen. And I do have something for you. There's part of the story you've yet to hear," Gran said, rising and squeezing Gwen's shoulder as she walked down the hall to the sitting room. Gwen heard her opening a drawer in her desk, but she zoned out as her mind skidded through all the knowledge she held now. Imagine a childhood fairy story turning out to be real! It was almost too much excitement for Gwen to bear, and she bounced in her seat yet again.

"After the fae disappeared, one lingered. I've not told you this, but she gave me a gift for you. One for when the time was right, she said." Gran held out a small box, coated in crystals and jewels, with a paper rolled and tied with a bow.

"This is stunning," Gwen breathed, placing the box gently

in front of her, marveling at how the light bounced off every gem at once, making it seem like a disco ball of a box. It was odd, but she could feel the energy pulse from it, as though what lay within was meant for her. Gwen shook her head at her foolishness.

"As was the woman. I swear she was different than the other fae." Gran laughed at herself. "Listen to me, talking like I know all about the fae. But she was different, I swear it. She had this glow around her and when she spoke it was like angels singing or flowers blooming… just this beautiful tone that almost resonated through you. Perhaps I only heard it in my mind, maybe she never even spoke out loud. But all she said is that you were meant for me and that, when the time was right, I should give you this gift. I asked how I would tell when the right moment came, and she promised I would know. In seconds she disappeared and I was left holding a laughing baby and this beautiful jeweled box."

"What did you tell people when you got back?"

"I made up a story that a long-lost relative had died and left you an orphan, and I was next of kin. Surprisingly, no one ever really questioned me on it. I think the fae helped that along," Gran admitted, sitting back to smile at Gwen. "Well? Are you going to open it?"

"Of course!" Gwen exclaimed. She first picked up the scroll, carefully untying the ribbon that held it closed. Unrolling the paper, she tilted her head in confusion at the line on the paper.

"Well? Oh, look at me, I'm all aflutter," Gran laughed.

"It says, 'Fire and Ice, Song by Song, Day by Night, One follows along.'"

"That… I don't know what to say to that. I'm not sure what that would mean," Gran said.

Gwen just smiled at her. "I'm certain there will be a lot that doesn't make sense. We'll figure it out, I just can feel it. In my comic books, there is always some clue and then a quest. I'm sure there's more to the story here," Gwen said, then gasped as she opened the hinged lid of the box.

"Oh, these are perfect... just completely me. They are meant for me," Gwen said. She was unsure how she knew that, but she had no doubt.

Two cuff bracelets lay nestled on purple satin. The metal was gold, but antiqued gold, hammered out and etched with symbols unknown to Gwen. In the center of one was a stone of icy blue, almost white, and in the other, a stone of the deepest red.

"Fire and ice," Gwen breathed, pulling them out to show her gran.

"Oh... oh my." Gran's hands hovered over the cuffs, but then she pulled back. "I feel as though I shouldn't touch them. They're meant for you. You're right about that."

Gwen nodded, not questioning Gran, and slid the first one – the ice – onto her right wrist. The metal twisted, morphing, and became a closed circle on her wrist – no longer a cuff.

"Did you see that?!" Gwen exclaimed, holding her wrist up in awe. "It's a bracelet now. I don't think it is meant to come off."

"Thank goodness you like them, then," Gran said, causing Gwen to laugh.

"Thank goodness indeed," Gwen said, repeating the movement with the other arm, laughing again when the cuff became a solid bracelet.

"They really are stunning. And they just suit you. I wonder what they're meant for? Or if they mean something – maybe you're a princess!" Gran exclaimed, then covered her face with her hands. "Listen to me... I'm getting just as caught up as you."

"It's not a bad thought to have. Maybe I *am* a princess. Wouldn't that be something?" Gwen chuckled, lifting her wrists to admire the way the light caught the bracelets. They weren't heavy at all; in fact, if it weren't for the power coursing through them, she probably wouldn't notice she was wearing them at all.

"Do you think they would have done the same if you had switched what wrist you wore them on?" Gran asked.

"Fire was meant for my left... my heart," Gwen said automatically, then paused. How did she know that?

"Hmm. I wonder if fire means passion. Oh... like love! Maybe you'll find love?" Gran asked, excitement lacing her voice.

Gwen picked up a cookie and shoved it in her mouth before she could say anything. For the first thing that had entered her mind when Gran had brought up love was none other than an insufferable god of a man – Lochlain himself. And even she knew that fairytales didn't work with princesses like herself. Loch was not meant for her.

CHAPTER 10

"So this is our Protector?" Bianca asked, raising an eyebrow at the sulking man who lounged in the corner of the all but empty pub, his boots propped on a chair, his eyes cast out the window. The few people who did enter the pub were wise enough to give the leather-clad man a wide berth, and Bianca didn't blame them. Who wanted to talk to a cranky, overly-muscled man?

Well, apparently some girls found the attitude attractive. Bianca sniffed as a blonde approached Loch, but he quickly shrugged her hand off his arm and dismissed her.

"Aye, he's the one," Seamus said, taking a sip of his pint.

"At least he's not a man-whore," Bianca said, watching him fend off another woman who dared to approach him. "What's with these women anyway? Can't they see he looks like an absolute pain in the arse to deal with?"

"I think it's exactly his arse they're thinking of, my love," Seamus said, patting her leg.

"No brains in any of them, then," Bianca said, dismissing the women and smiling up at Seamus.

"You can't be telling me you don't think he's attractive?" Seamus asked, tilting his head at her in question.

Bianca looked over at Loch once again, studying his build, his moody eyes, and angular face.

"Aye, I can see the appeal, if that's your type. He's not hard on the eyes, I suppose. But all that muscle and attitude? No, thank you. I like my men all lean muscle and whip-smart brains. I've never been one for the brawny romance novel types."

"I can romance the heck out of you, woman," Seamus growled, burying his face in her neck and making her giggle as he dropped a kiss at the sensitive spot on her collarbone.

"Aye, you can at that," Bianca agreed. "I've eyes only for you, my love."

"Good, then you won't force me to prove my manhood against the Hulk over there." Seamus smiled again and took another sip from his pint, nodding his thanks to the waitress as she dropped a plate of fish and chips in front of him.

"Tell me about the Seeker," Bianca said, biting a chip and then glaring down at it before realizing she hadn't doused it in vinegar yet. Grabbing the bottle, she poured a generous portion and waited for Seamus to speak.

"I think we're going to like this one," Seamus said, then filled Bianca in on the ice incident until she was doubled over in laughter.

"Must you tell everyone?" A shadow fell over her and Bianca straightened to see Loch glowering down at them.

"Not everyone. Just the love of my life. Bianca, this is Lochlain, a highly esteemed fae sorcerer. His magick is mighty, though his attitude be sour," Seamus said, biting back a smile as Loch's glare deepened.

"It's pleased I am to be making your acquaintance,"

Bianca said sweetly, dimpling up at him until the lines in his face eased a bit. Charm usually worked well for her.

"I don't quite see why it is you're both following me," Loch said, his voice raspy, his eyes always scanning the room.

"Oh, you know, the fate of the world and all that," Bianca said, taking another chip from the plate. "And because the Goddess Danu asked us to."

"You've met her?" Loch said, showing actual interest for the first time.

"Aye, a couple times now. It's quite a sight each time. I have to admit I do get a little fan-girl when I see her. It's just… wow, you know?" Bianca thumped her ample chest and laughed. "Just kind of hits you in the chest and you can't really breathe, but you don't *want* to breathe or speak or miss a minute of it."

"She's a powerful presence, that's the truth of it," Seamus agreed.

"She's not my favorite at the moment," Loch said, and both Seamus and Bianca paused.

"Erm… why would that be?" Bianca raised her chin.

"That's my business and not yours. I'll deal with Danu when I finish this silly quest. For now, let's find the Seeker and get on the way. There's no point in sitting here and waiting for more Domnua," Loch said, staring at their food pointedly.

"A body needs to eat," Seamus said cheerfully, taking a bite of his fish. "I suggest you do so as well. You never know where we'll be taken next. And things can change in an instant. One thing we've learned already is to take the small moments of joy and comfort when they come. Fate's wind is a fickle one."

Loch studied them for a moment before sighing and pulling up a chair, signaling to the waitress.

"Fair enough. You might as well fill me in on the events that have transpired so far. I want the full details – leave nothing out."

"Oh, yes sir. Please, sir, can we do this for you, sir?" Bianca said, her voice dripping with sarcasm. This man definitely rubbed her the wrong way.

Loch scrubbed a hand over his face and blew out a frustrated sigh.

"I'm used to giving orders. I'll try to phrase things more appropriately," Loch said.

Bianca waited a beat, then, realizing that was a close to an apology as she would get, she shrugged. "Settle in, my friend. It's story time."

They kept their heads low, talking quietly as Loch learned of the two prior quests before his.

And in doing so, they missed the rain that began to fall... the Domnua curled in the drops... silver balls of fate bursting on the streets.

CHAPTER 11

*G*wen all but skipped down the darkened street, paying no mind when a gentle rain began to fall. Pulling the hood of her cardigan over her head, she hummed Queen's

"Bohemian Rhapsody" as she bounced along, lost in thoughts of fairytale worlds and magickal powers.

She'd left Gran with the promise she'd call her tomorrow – and an extra long hug to reassure Gran that she was her family, and nothing and no one would ever change that. As she'd told her repeatedly, Gran had given her the best life, and love was love. Blood or not, the bond that bound Gran and Gwen was ironclad as far as Gwen was concerned.

Gwen glanced down at the bracelets on her wrists, the ruby red of the fire stone gleaming in the pale light of the streetlamp. She couldn't wait to test the bracelets out – to see if they actually held the power that she swore she could feel humming through them. Perhaps they were just a way of keeping her connected to her birth family, she mused, as the rain began to intensify.

Perhaps if she had let the earlier run-in with the silvery bad fae rattle her more, Gwen would have been more alert. It was only luck that made her pause in mid-stride to consider something, and thus narrowly miss the arc of a blade that should have been a killing blow. Acting purely on instinct, Gwen whirled, her arms up, and ice flew in shards from her hands, miniature ice daggers finding their marks in the three fae who all looked down in disbelief at the shards buried deep in their chests, silver liquid pouring rapidly from them.

"Back off!" Gwen shouted, stepping slowly back, her arms crossed in front of her. But she was speaking to air, for the three had dissolved quickly to puddles on the street, the rain claiming their blood.

"There. Took care of that all on my own, didn't I? I won't be needing the likes of Loch, that's for damn sure," Gwen said, ignoring the pounding in her chest. So what if she had some adrenaline coursing through her? It wasn't every day she had numerous attacks on her life. Pausing to look at where her arm throbbed, Gwen cursed when she saw a rip in her cardigan. This was one of her favorite sweaters and now Gran would have to patch it for her. Annoyed all around, Gwen turned to go.

And squeaked when she was met with a wall of silver men, materializing seemingly from each raindrop that fell, hundreds upon hundreds of them, all staring at her with menace.

"Guys, I'm certain we can work something out here," Gwen stammered, her pulse kicking into high gear, a bead of sweat trickling through her hairline. "Just tell me what you want from me and I'll give it to you." As she spoke, Gwen gestured with her hands and as one the men gasped, all eyes on the bracelets on her wrists. In seconds they were whispering to each other.

"These? Is that what you want? I'd, uh, give them to you, but I'm certain they are meant to stay with me. So, something else then?" Gwen stammered, trying to back up, but realizing too late that she was surrounded.

And still the rain fell.

"Gwenith who dances with fairies," Gwen whispered to herself, circling, circling, trying to force herself to think past the panic that wanted to rise and overtake her thoughts. "You're of magickal blood. What would a warrior princess do?"

One fae stepped forward and flashed her a cocky grin, inadvertently giving Gwen something to home her rage on.

"Got it. Be a badass and die fighting." Gwen steeled her nerves and smiled back at the fae, giving it a come-hither look. Or, at least, it was what she thought a come-hither look would be, but it was probably more of a grimace coming from her. The fae paused, which was just enough time for Gwen to launch her attack.

"I love you, Gran!" Gwen shrieked, inexplicably, and raising her arms, she blasted as many ice shards as she could, swinging in a circle, like some sort of sub-automatic machine gun of ice, taking more joy than she would have thought possible in the number of fae that dropped in front of her.

Still, the rain persisted.

Knowing she was but one, that they were too many, Gwen kept icing, praying her nearly untested magick would hold. When the circle drew tight, the fae too numerous for her, Gwen closed her eyes.

"Eyes open, missy. You can't fight a battle like that," Loch drawled from beside her, carelessly and far too easily dropping fae left and right with whatever magick he was wringing from those incredible hands of his.

Incredible hands of his? Gwen shook her head. She must still be alive if she was admiring Loch's muscular forearms.

"Nice of you to show up," she muttered.

Loch cast a glare at her.

"It seems you take great joy in turning down my help. Tell me again why I should be assisting you?" Loch asked, his eyes on hers while he easily deflected the advance of the fae, his magick seemingly keeping them away from her while also dropping them in their tracks. She wondered briefly if he'd concocted some sort of force-field around her.

"Sorry about that." Gwen cleared her throat. "I don't take well to strangers being rude to me."

"If you think that was rude, we're going to have one hell of a time ahead of us."

Gwen's thoughts tripped over the idea of them being an "us," but she couldn't think too much about it as the rain continued to fall, each drop exploding into a silvery fae who bounded to his feet, ready to attack.

"Can't you stop the rain or something?" a voice asked in irritation. Gwen swung around, shocked to see a round blonde cheerfully stabbing silver fae as easily as if she were picking flowers for a bouquet.

"She's got a point," another voice said and Gwen whirled the other way to see a lanky red-headed man calmly delivering killing blows with a bow and arrow. The four of them stood, backs to each other, and patiently picked off the inner circle of fae that never seemed to end.

"Um, who are these people?" Gwen asked Loch over her shoulder – a shoulder which, she noticed, was growing increasingly cold.

"Bianca's my name," the blonde called cheerfully, "and that handsome ginger right there is all mine, so don't think about it, mmmkay? We're your team, so to speak. Your squad, your army, your back-up. Whatever you want to call us. We're sent by the goddess to help you on your quest."

"My… my quest," Gwen stammered. She dropped her arm, which now screamed in pain, but kept the other one up, still feebly trying to shoot ice at the fae.

"Aye, to find the Spear of Lugh. Or the Spear of Truth. The Spear of Light. It's got all sorts of names. Either way, it's yours to be finding, and we are but your minions," Bianca said, delightfully stabbing another fae right in the heart.

"The spear?" In that moment, a lightheadedness swept over her and Gwen realized she was about to faint. "My… my arm."

That was the last thing she knew before she crumpled face-down in a puddle of silver blood and rivulets of rain.

CHAPTER 12

*G*wen blinked awake, like a TV turning on, going so suddenly from unconscious to conscious that she barely dared to breathe. Had she been taken captive? Was this what death felt like?

If so, it was a surprisingly comfortable death, Gwen thought, feeling snuggly warm on a bed, her only pressing need that of using the toilet.

"Hey, sleepy-head." The blonde woman – Bianca, Gwen reminded herself – leaned over the bed and smiled at her.

"Hi. Um, did we get captured? What happened?" Gwen asked, swallowing against the dryness in her throat. She wondered if she'd been snoring while she was passed out, then mentally groaned at the thought of snoring around the handsome Lochlain. Maybe he'd disappeared with the fae? Perhaps this was all some weird dream.

"Finally, you're awake," Loch said, stepping to the bed and running a cursory glance over Gwen. She sighed. No such luck on the whole this-is-just-a-dream thing, Gwen thought, and then almost blushed when she realized she must look a fright.

And why did she care how she looked? Gwen reminded herself again that men like Loch never looked at women like her.

"Nice bedside manner, Doc." Bianca shot Loch a glare and put her hand to Gwen's forehead to check for fever.

"What happened?" Gwen asked, gratefully accepting the glass of water that Bianca handed her.

"You were wounded. A slice in your arm. Fae blades are cursed with dark magick, so you must be careful not to get hit," Bianca gently admonished Gwen. "It takes strong magick to heal you as quickly as we were able to. You've Loch to thank for that one."

Gwen's eyes met his tawny ones, and she wished she could read what lay in the depths of them.

"Aye, then it's beholden to you I am," Gwen said, smiling at Loch.

"No matter," Loch said, brushing the healing off as if it were as minor as picking up a napkin she'd dropped. "I'm just grateful I was able to heal you on my own merits this time."

"What do you mean, 'this time'? Was there someone you weren't able to heal?" Gwen asked, and was shocked to see a bolt of rage flicker over Loch's face before he schooled his expression.

"Let's just say that I'm grateful I didn't have to go to the same extremes as I once did in the past," Loch bit out, and Gwen wondered what it was that made him so furious. Shouldn't he be happy that healing her from what could have been a mortal fae wound had come so easily to him? Men and their egos, Gwen thought, shaking her head before turning back to Bianca.

"Where are we?"

"We've left the village. Too many Domnua knew where we were. It's really best to keep moving," Bianca said, her voice trailing after her as she moved across the room to a small kitchenette in the corner, where a pot bubbled on the stove. Gwen propped herself up more to take in her surroundings. Her bed was tucked under an alcove in what seemed to be a single-room cottage.

Seamus stoked a small potbellied stove, the flames offering warmth in the small room, and Loch sat down in an armchair, his face stormy. At the stove, Bianca poured what looked to be soup into a bowl and brought it over to Gwen's bedside. "Here. Eat this and let's have ourselves a bit of a chat," she said.

As if on cue, Seamus drew Loch into a conversation, giving the women a little bit of privacy.

"Thank you. I'm famished," Gwen admitted, spooning up the vegetable stew and trying not to glance across the room at Loch, who was still glowering.

"He's handsome, isn't he?" Bianca asked, catching Gwen's stolen glance.

"Um, yeah, are you kidding me? He looks like one of the superheros in my comic books. I bet every woman within meters of him stops to come talk to him. He's every man's worst nightmare and every woman's secret dream. Handsome doesn't even do him justice," Gwen gushed.

Bianca drew back in surprise before laughing at Gwen. "So you fancy him already, then?"

"What?" Gwen almost dropped the bowl of soup, then laughed. "Me? No. Men like him don't go for women like me. They go for, like... the showstoppers. All glitz and glamor. Women who glide places and wear towering icepick stiletto heels. I'm more of a run-into-the-wall and wear t-shirts type of girl. It would be a match made in hell, that it would be. I'm cool with that. Much easier to conduct a quest without romance getting in the way," Gwen said, scooping up more soup before pointing the spoon at Bianca. "Speaking of quests, care to fill a girl in?"

"Aye, I have so much to tell you – but first, I just have to say this," Bianca said, reaching out to pat Gwen's arm. "I think you're stunning. You just aren't seeing yourself as others do."

Heat crept up Gwen's cheeks and she cursed her fair skin once again for giving away her emotions. "That's sweet of you, but I'm comfortable with knowing that I'm passably attractive at best. Otherwise more men would've taken notice of me in the village or made more of an attempt to date me," Gwen shrugged, uncomfortable with talking about her looks when they had so many more interesting things to speak of, like magick and murdering fae.

"I'm thinking it's because they were too intimidated by you," Bianca said softly, and Gwen let out a peal of laughter that had both men glancing their way.

"That's a thought, isn't it? Not likely, but you sure are a doll," Gwen chuckled again, delighted to have Bianca along on whatever quest this was.

"I think you underestimate yourself. But that's all I'll say about that. As for the quest, have you heard of the four trea-sures – the great treasures of the god cities?"

"Aye, I have, at that. Legends and myths abound around them. Great fun to read about," Gwen said, then paused, real-ization hitting her like a ton of bricks. "Wait – you're saying the treasures are real? The spear? That's mine to find? Why are they lost? Wait… they're real?"

"They are as real as that spoon you're holding," Bianca smiled, leaning back to cross her arms over her chest. "And they're missing because centuries ago, a curse was laid upon Ireland by the bad fae."

"The Domnua," Gwen said, testing out the word on her tongue and finding she didn't like it.

"Correct. Goddess Danu's bitchy sister is their queen mum, if you will," Bianca said. "If the Danula – the good guys" – Bianca pointed to Seamus and Loch – "haven't found the four treasures before the time is up, the Domnua will rise up and inherit the world."

"Oh, so no big deal," Gwen said faintly.

"Have faith. We're doing good so far, with two of the treasures found and kicking right along. Plus, you've already found your magick and you've got a high and mighty sorcerer as your Protector, so you're good to go," Bianca said, excitement flashing across her pretty face.

Gwen tried to reconcile the pretty blonde in the sweater set sitting across from her with the woman who had cheerfully murdered fae. She found herself struggling to make the connection. Though she supposed most wouldn't think of her as a murderer, either, and hadn't she killed her own fair share of fae as well?

"My… my Protector?" Gwen asked, casting a look over at Loch again.

"That's right. It's quite an honor, too. In each generation there are Seekers – Na Sirtheior and Protectors. The fae know who the Protectors are, and families are quite proud if one of theirs is chosen to protect. But this round of Seekers seems to have no prior knowledge of the quests. I'm going to guess you were probably an orphan of sorts, or adopted? That seems to be a theme here."

"Gran," Gwen breathed, fear racing up her so quickly that she almost dropped the bowl of soup she held. "I have to get to Gran. Make sure she's safe." Gwen sat up and tried to swing her legs over the side of the bed, desperate now to find a phone or go back to the village to find Gran.

"Loch took care of her. You have to listen to me," Bianca said sharply, putting her hands on Gwen's shoulders to hold her down. "She is safe."

Gwen read the truth in Bianca's eyes, but still needed to hear it from Loch.

"Is that true? Gran is safe?" Gwen asked, interrupting the conversation across the room.

Loch ran his eyes over Gwen. She nearly blushed when she realized she was wearing only a tank top, but the sheet was covering the rest of her body. Then he nodded at her.

"She's at my village. A magickal one that nobody knows of. The fae reside there and it is guarded by the Goddess Danu herself. There is no safer place for her in this world. Plus, she seemed delighted by all the fae who swooped in to fawn over her and ask questions. It seems they are just as curious as she is."

"That sounds like Gran. She loves telling me the story of how I once danced with fae," Gwen mused.

Loch came to a stand so fast she almost gasped. "What is this story exactly?"

"Oh… it's just a… well, I guess it's not," Gwen said, stuttering a bit as she realized it wasn't just a fairytale. Quickly relaying the story, she watched Loch's expression for any clues as to what it might mean.

"The bracelets – may I hold them?" Loch asked, though

she could read the struggle on his face when he asked instead of commanding her to hand them over.

"No. They are mine. I'm not certain I can even take them off. When I put them on, they morphed and locked up. I think they're on there for good now," Gwen said, jumping a little when Loch took her wrist in his hand, turning it so he could read the writing on the bracelet. Gwen tried to ignore the caress of his fingers on her skin, his touch sending heat trailing lazily up her arm.

"You can read them," Bianca said, tilting her head to study Loch as he examined Gwen's bracelets.

"Aye."

"What do they say?" Gwen asked.

Loch dropped her hand as quickly as he'd taken it and stormed from the room, the door banging behind him.

"The man has a flair for the dramatic," Seamus said from where he sat on the couch, tuning his fiddle. "I kind of like it. It keeps things interesting."

Interesting, indeed, Gwen thought and brushed her hand over her skin where she still felt the imprint of his touch.

He might be protecting her safety, but he was also protecting some very deep secrets.

*a*n hour passed and still Loch had not returned. Gwen shrugged it off, refusing to let herself be too drawn in by the enigmatic Protector. Instead, she passed the time playing a lazy game of cards with Seamus and Bianca, while getting up to speed on what the last Seekers had accomplished.

"From everything you're telling me, it's not going to be an easy road," she said, sighing as she folded her cards, losing another hand to the grinning Seamus.

"Ah, well, if it was easy, the payoff wouldn't be so great now, would it?" Bianca asked. "There's something wildly satisfying about knowing you've busted your arse to achieve something and actually getting it. Feels good, you know?"

"I'll be agreeing with you on that one." Gwen grinned at her. "Plus, if it was easy, the spear would have been found by now anyway. I don't think we're meant to be able to just stumble upon it on a wander-about."

"That's the truth of it. It'll be found when it is meant to be found, unless the Domnua have their way," Seamus said, leaning back to stretch his arms over his head, a yawn escaping his mouth.

"Why don't you both rest? Seems you've had some long shifts keeping an eye on me. I'm sure Loch has protected this place, so you can rest a little easier. As for me, I'm hoping for a quick nip into the shower so I can feel human again and then I'll rest as well. Tomorrow's another day to fight for the good of the world," Gwen said.

Bianca smiled, her cheeks dimpling in delight. "I have to say, I'm delighted to be working with a Seeker that's as positive as I am. No sense in being down in the doldrums about such matters. We'll be figuring this out together and we'll take each day as it comes." Bianca nodded, the matter settled, and she and Seamus stood to pull the mattress out from the folded couch. Belatedly, Gwen realized – if she got the bedroom and they had the couch, where would Loch sleep?

Not like the man seemed interested in spending time around her, let alone sleeping with her, Gwen reminded herself as she waved goodnight to Bianca and Seamus and assessed her luggage situation.

Or lack thereof, Gwen thought, her eyes trailing around the room to land on the torn cardigan she'd been wearing earlier. With her serviceable boots, pants, t-shirt, support tank, and underwear, that completed her wardrobe options. Spying her purse, she gave a silent prayer of thanks to Bianca for remembering to grab it on the way to wherever Loch had them squirreled away. Picking it up, she rummaged around until she found her comb and a small tube of lip balm. Never one for wearing much makeup, she really only cared about being able to detangle the mass of hair currently in a knot on her head.

"That's about it for you, Gwennie. You'll just need to turn

your underwear inside out and perhaps pick up a pair or two as we go along," Gwen muttered to herself, stripping and hanging her clothes on a hook by the tiny shower. Praying for warm water, she unwound her hair and waited, sending up a silent thanks when a puff of steam floated over the glass shower door.

Grateful for a moment alone, Gwen stepped under the stream of water, letting it pour over her head, and just closed her eyes as the warmth enveloped her. She braced her hands on the wall, happy as she could be in the moment, and thought about all the events that had transpired that day. Even though most women would probably be terrified if a pack of evil fae were hunting them, Gwen couldn't help but feel a trickle of excitement lance through her.

For once, her life was interesting. Not that she wasn't content – oh no; she loved her life. But it was predictable and settled, and this... well, this was something fascinating and new with twists and turns and all the beautiful magick to learn about. Aye, it was hard not to be excited, Gwen thought, and began to hum as she ran the comb through her hair, happy enough to begin to sing – quietly, though – as she struggled with a particularly difficult knot in her hair.

Gwen's voice, a secret but to her and her gran, filled the small shower stall, the rich tones reverberating back at her and, as always, filling her with joy and yet making her ache for something she didn't quite understand, but oh so desperately craved.

And when the bracelets at her wrists began to sing – matching her song, all but deafening her in the beauty of the sounds that rang from them – lust, full and robust, slammed into her so that she clutched the side of the shower door, nearly crumbling to the floor as wave after wave of pure pleasure swept through her.

Gwen could only gasp, holding on for dear life, while pleasure threatened to drag her down into its beauty and anguish as an age-old craving for intimacy and love rose up and wound through her.

The door to the bathroom crashed open. Blue eyes met tawny ones, and Gwen raised her chin in challenge.

Then she sagged against the shower wall as Loch cursed, slamming the door behind him as he left, little pops of pleasure still working their way through her body. Gwen had no idea what had just happened with her bracelets, but she wasn't certain she'd survive another rush of whatever it was.

Shaking, she looked down at her wrists.

"No more singing, Gwen."

CHAPTER 14

"*I*s she okay? What was that?" Bianca demanded the minute Loch swept from the bathroom.

"She's fine. More than fine, I promise you that," Loch said, moving from the bedroom to pace the main room.

"That song… wowza," Seamus said from behind Bianca, running his hands through hair that was already standing on end. His face was flushed and his eyes kept straying to Bianca, and Loch knew exactly what was on his mind. It was what was on his own mind as well.

"I'll be outside. Do not let her sing. Understood?" Loch hoped the look he leveled at them was dangerous enough to scare the two into following his orders, and judging from how they both nodded meekly at him, it had worked. Cursing once again, Loch slammed from the cottage to pace outside, where a soft mist cooled his burning skin.

He needed to touch her with every ounce of his being.

Forcing his libido to calm down, Loch stalked the land, working his way through a spell that he used immediately on himself – the magickal world's version of a cold shower.

He'd been outside, stoically walking the perimeter of his magick and checking his wards meticulously, when the song had gone up, spearing straight to his heart, his loins, every last particle in his body. Loch didn't even know how he'd gotten to her so fast. It was as though the song had carried him blindly through the house until he'd found her.

Loch clenched his jaw as the image of her filled his mind, his fingers curling in his need to reach out and touch her.

Oh, she'd been beauty beyond even what he had imagined. Loch was grateful now for the frumpy way she dressed, for if Gwen had even an ounce of an idea of how to really dress her body – well, no man would stand a chance, in Loch's opinion. Water from the shower had dripped down to slip over her lush body – curves in all the right places, her ivory skin pink from the steam. And flushed from something more – pleasure that came not just from her song, but from somewhere deep inside her. When she'd raised her chin to challenge him, her blue eyes huge in her face, her breath coming in soft pants – like a woman experiencing true pleasure for the first time – it had taken all of Loch's training and infamous control to leave her.

He'd wanted nothing more than to step into the shower and wrap his hands around the mass of hair that curled wetly almost to her waist, pull her to him until his lips could taste that mouth that begged to be kissed. His hands had ached to touch, his lips to taste, his body to claim – claim what he now knew was his to have.

Loch gripped his fists tightly and continued his perimeter check, forcing his mind away from the demanding beauty of a naked and deliciously wet Gwen. It would test his very last dredges of control to protect her on this quest and to keep her safe from harm.

He just wasn't sure anymore whether he was protecting her from the Domnua – or from himself.

CHAPTER 15

*G*wen stayed in the shower until hot water ran out, and even then she stayed a moment longer, allowing her skin to pucker in the cold and hoping against hope that the shock of the icy water would tamp down the feelings of lust that still threatened to overtake her.

What the heck had happened? It wasn't the first time she had sung in the shower, and nothing like that had ever happened before. It had to be her new bracelets, Gwen surmised, as she finally left the shower stall and gingerly picked up the towel she'd placed on the toilet. Twitching when the soft cotton met her skin, Gwen forced herself not to moan as she dried herself off, the touch of the fabric once again sending trickles of pleasure through her.

If these were some sort of lust bracelets, Gwen wasn't sure she wanted them. Talk about distracting, she thought as she quickly dressed and wrapped the towel around her mass of hair. Quietly easing the door open, Gwen stepped out into the bedroom. The door was now closed, a small lamp by the bed providing the only light. A low chuckle and the unmistakable sounds of pleasure sounded from the main room and Gwen blushed, quickly realizing what Seamus and Bianca were up to. Had her song done that to them?

It had certainly done something to her.

Gwen sat on the corner of the bed and looked down at the bracelets, gleaming dully in the light from the lamp. She felt awakened somehow, in a way she hadn't been before – almost more womanly or more powerful. When Loch had burst into the bathroom she should have shrieked in outrage. Instead, she'd lifted her chin and all but invited the man into the shower with her. For one agonizing instant, she'd thought Loch would meet her challenge head-on, but then he'd done the smart thing and stormed out. Gwen didn't blame him in the least. There was no reason for them to be mixing business and pleasure. Especially considering the fact that she was untouched goods. It was best she didn't try out that particular life experience when the fate of the world hung in her hands.

Or was it the perfect time? A little voice niggled in her brain, and she rolled her eyes and leaned back on the bed, crossing her arms behind her head. *You may die on this quest – do you want to die not knowing the pleasures of intimacy?* Gwen sighed once more, forcing the voice down, and instead turned her mind to the song.

Music had always been a part of her life, and she'd been drawn to it at a young age. It was not uncommon for the Irish to play an instrument or join in song. Sessions in the pub were a common thing. Gwen was fairly certain most people in her village either played an instrument or sang a tune on occasion – neither of which Gwen did. The villagers had finally put it down to shyness and stopped pushing Gwen to join their sessions. Instead, she'd steal away to a corner, mouthing the words of the songs, her foot tapping to the beat.

She couldn't completely recall the incident that had stopped her from singing in public – aye, she'd most likely blocked it out, Gwen thought – but she did remember that it had been the only time Gran had ever yelled at her. Later, Gwen had been punished and made to swear to never sing again except under Gran's supervision. And so Gwen had quietly kept her voice to herself, knowing something was different or wrong with it, and would only sing around Gran. When she did sing, Gran would smile and tell her how beautiful it was – but always after she'd wrung the promise from Gwen to never sing around others.

As it was the only promise Gran had ever asked of her, she'd stuck to it.

Now she wondered just what had happened and what Gran knew – and what other people heard when she sang. To her, it sounded pretty enough, but for all she knew it could sound like snakes hissing.

Contemplating her bracelets once more, Gwen finally allowed herself to think about what she'd been purposely trying to distract herself from – the look of pure longing on Loch's face when he'd seen her.

Rolling over, Gwen squeezed the pillow to her. Oh, but a secret part of her had always wanted a man to look at her that way – as though he could devour her in one bite. Gwen imagined he probably could, since he was so large. Her mind slipped into dangerous territory when she considered his size, and her entire body flushed with heat once more. Lochlain was danger, through and through, and she'd do best to remember that.

This new Gwen wasn't afraid of danger anymore.

CHAPTER 16

"So is anyone going to talk about what happened last night?" Bianca asked the next morning after a breakfast of oatmeal and fruit, where her every attempt at conversation had been met with a wall of silence.

Gwen choked on the piece of apple she was eating while studiously ignoring Loch's hulking presence across the table from her. Damn, but the man's energy seemed to radiate as though he was crackling with barely contained power. It was almost exhausting for her to ignore him.

"All good there, tiger?" Seamus asked as he cheerfully pounded her back. Of course he had something to be cheerful about – he'd had his fun with Bianca last night.

"Ahem. Yes, all good," Gwen said, clearing her throat and refusing to look at Loch.

"Well, I mean, come on!" Bianca exclaimed, grabbing her empty bowl and moving toward the sink to wash it. "It was like a force of nature – one of the most intensely beautiful songs I have ever heard. It was all I could do not to go running in to listen to you. Though someone else did."

Gwen flushed as she felt heat trickle through her again, thinking of the challenge she'd presented to Loch last night – and how it had been denied.

"Aye, I did. And I'll be apologizing for that," Loch said, clearing his throat and nodding curtly in her direction. "'Twas quite rude of me."

"Ah... that's fine. It's fine. No matter," Gwen stuttered and shoved a spoonful of oatmeal in her mouth to stop whatever else was going to rush out of it.

"Did something happen?" Bianca demanded, hands on her hips. "No way did something happen. You were out of there in a shot. No time. Unless he kissed you. Did he kiss you?" Bianca looked between them both, her head swiveling like a referee at a tennis match.

"No!" Gwen exclaimed. Could this get any more embarrassing?

"Why not? I almost kissed her meself. That's a mighty powerful voice you've got there," Seamus said.

Gwen quickly looked at Bianca to see if she was jealous, but the blonde only nodded along in agreement. "'Tis true, Gwen. I've never heard the likes of it before. You could be famous! Have you thought of singing professionally?"

"I wouldn't recommend that," Loch said.

Bianca turned to look at him as she cleared Seamus's bowl from the table. "And why not? You heard it for yourself. It's amazing."

"I wouldn't. I promised my gran I wouldn't sing," Gwen said, shaking her head and interrupting so she wouldn't have to hear Loch's answer.

"And why's that?" Bianca asked. "The woman's a fool if she told you not to sing."

"I'm not quite sure. I don't remember all of the details,

but from what Gran tells me it was an incident when I was a child. I was singing and there was a bit of a car accident along where I was walking. It wasn't like anyone died, but it was enough of a pile-up that Gran made me promise not to sing. She said it could be distracting to some. Ever since then, I've been scared of hurting someone again, so I typically just sing quietly to myself. I'm not sure why it even got so loud, to be honest. I think it's these." Gwen held up the bracelets.

"You think they amplified your voice?" Bianca asked, head tilted as she studied the bracelets.

"They unlocked the power within her," Loch finally grunted, and they all stopped to stare at him.

"But I already unlocked the whole shards of ice thing, remember?" Gwen asked, beginning to feel annoyed that the man clearly knew more about her than she did. It wasn't a comfortable feeling, someone knowing secrets about her that she'd yet to discover. In fact, it made her downright irritable.

"What else aren't you telling us, O great and admirable sorcerer?" Bianca asked, sarcasm dripping from every word.

Loch sighed, leaning back to cross his arms behind his head as he stared at the wooden rafters crisscrossing the ceiling. Momentarily distracted by the way his shirt pulled tight across the muscles of his chest, Gwen almost missed what he said next.

Almost.

"Gwen's a siren."

CHAPTER 17

"*A* ... a siren," Gwen croaked, the breath leaving her body in one big whoosh of surprise.

Bianca squealed in delight, running around the table to squeeze Gwen's shoulders.

"A siren! That's so cool! I've always wanted to know more about the sirens. See? I told you how beautiful you are and you didn't believe me. You're a freaking siren! The most beautiful, that is! Your song can enchant anyone. Oh, this is so neat. Can you sing again? I'd love to hear it and feel if it pulls me the same way it does the men. Do you think you'd be able to resist her, Seamus? What would happen? Wait, do you kill the men after you've had them?" Bianca chattered on, beyond delighted with this development.

Gwen's mouth worked, attempting to form a word, while her brain refused to process what she'd just heard.

A siren. The mythological beauties of the deep that lured sailors to their deaths, Gwen thought dumbly, as far away as possible from what she believed herself to be. A giggle escaped her mouth, surprising her, and she swallowed down another that wanted to follow it. It was all just too... impossible. For years she'd been someone men barely paid attention to, and now Loch was trying to tell her that she could lure them to their deathbeds with her looks and a song?

It was madness.

"Sure and it was a lovely song and all – no harm meant, Gwen," Seamus said, his cheeks flushing a bit. "But if it's all the same to you, I'd like to not be testing whether I can resist it or not. Or, you know, that little bit after, where she tears men limb from limb once she's finished with them."

Gwen laughed this time, a full-bodied laugh that shook her very core, and in moments she was doubled over, wiping tears from her eyes.

"I think that's probably a wise idea, Seamus," Loch said dryly, keeping one eye on Gwen as tears continued to run down her cheeks.

"Since this one can't talk, tell me what you know about her. It's only fair," Bianca demanded, sticking a finger in Loch's face. Gwen admired the fact that Bianca was clearly not intimidated by Lochlain's bulk.

"That's what I've been trying to figure out." Loch sighed and stood, surprising Gwen by taking his bowl to the sink and rinsing it out, drying it as he spoke. It was nice to see that he didn't deem doing the dishes as woman's work, Gwen thought, finally able to stop laughing as she waited for him to speak. "The bracelets are what's throwing me."

"What about them specifically? I saw you were able to read the writing. Seamus, can you?" Bianca asked. Gwen held her breath as Seamus took her wrist to examine the ice bracelet.

"No, I can't," Seamus said after squinting carefully down at the symbols wrought on the hammered gold.

"Why can you, then?" Bianca swiveled back to Loch.

"He's royalty. Which means… she likely is as well," Seamus said, his fingers drumming on the table as he thought it through. "There is a language that only the royal fae learn, so if Loch can read it, that means he's royalty. What's interesting to me is that the royal family are very particular about who knows this language, as well as how it is used. For Gwen to have bracelets with the language transcribed upon them would lead me to conclude that she is royalty as well."

For the second time in a matter of minutes, Gwen was rendered speechless as she once again tried to process a concept that was unfathomable to her. First a siren and now royalty?

"Are you saying I'm a fairy princess?" Gwen said, the words ending on a higher pitch as she questioned everything she knew about herself.

"I'm thinking so, though it would be nice if this one could be confirming it," Seamus said, and they all looked to Loch.

His cursory nod had Bianca squealing in delight and rushing around the room to put her arms around Gwen.

"Royalty! Och, this is amazing!"

"Should I call you 'your highness' then?" Seamus asked, dipping into a bow and making Gwen giggle once more.

"Enough," Loch said, his voice a low growl, and the frustration behind it caused the laughter around the table to die.

"Now, Loch. It's best to enjoy these moments. At any second, we could be back in battle," Bianca said. "Isn't that the point of all this? To appreciate the lighter moments in life to help us through the darker ones?"

"And while you giggle over fairy princesses, I worry that the target on Gwen's back has now quadrupled. The Domnua know what those bracelets mean. If they can kill royalty?

Well, that would be hugely motivating to them. They'll feel invincible and push even harder. Half of what's keeping them at bay is their fear. If they have a massive win, like killing Danula royalty? Well, I shudder to think about what a mess this battle will become."

"Way to be a buzzkill," Bianca muttered.

Gwen smiled at her. Though her anxiety had flared at the thought of the Domnua, it still didn't outweigh the excitement that coursed through her.

A fairy princess, and a siren, at that. It would take a while for all this to soak in, but learning this information made her sit a little straighter in her seat. A princess wouldn't slump.

"I have a question," Gwen asked, careful to only look at Loch briefly before turning to Bianca, who, she had learned yesterday, gave tours at Dublin University detailing Celtic myths and history. "If a siren kills a man after luring them – how did I come about, exactly? Or did my father die in my mother's arms after he impregnated her?"

"That is an excellent question. Because it seems to me that sirens were known for killing men – perhaps mating with them first – but rarely if ever did a man live after a siren had her way with him. Ultimately, it is believed that nothing good comes from answering a siren's call," Bianca mused.

Gwen flashed back to the night before, when she'd sung and not known what she'd done. Even though it hadn't been purposeful, she'd still instinctively challenged Loch when he'd burst through the door.

Which to her mind meant two things: Loch wasn't actually attracted to her – as she'd correctly assumed from the beginning – and he was capable of resisting a siren's call.

"Does the siren's song have to be sung with the intention to lure a victim?" Gwen asked, carefully looking away from

Loch. "I mean, is it any time I sing that I can potentially harm people, or do I need to intend to enchant them?"

"Ahhh, interesting thought. If a siren sings for the joy of singing, does she lure a man?" Bianca asked, steepling her fingers and leaning forward on the table with her brow creased as she thought.

"I'd say no. Though it was a mighty powerful song you were singing last night, I was able to resist rushing to you," Seamus said, his eyes on Loch. "But it was still powerful. I'd hate to think what would happen if you did sing with intention. And Loch was drawn to you, but then resisted. So I'm thinking you didn't pack your full wallop, if you will."

"Half-siren," Loch said, almost absently, as he sipped his tea. "A half-blood. It will be interesting to see where her powers lie. I've not heard tell of this in the books, but I have a direction to research now. I'll be back." With that, he shoved off, leaving them staring after him.

"I can't decide if I was just insulted or not," Gwen said, her nose wrinkled in disgust.

"Don't mind him. He's got a fancy for you and doesn't like it, is all," Bianca soothed.

Gwen laughed. "No chance. The man saw me naked and heard my supposed 'siren song' and he still didn't jump me. I think it's safe to say he's not interested."

CHAPTER 18

*I*t rankled just a bit, and perhaps more than she wanted to admit, Gwen thought as she stared out the window of the military-style SUV Loch had piled them into shortly after breakfast. Not that she wanted a relationship with a man like Loch, she reminded herself, but she'd be a liar if she said her mind didn't wander that way. The man was too handsome for his own good, though his attitude could use work. He'd returned after he'd stormed off at breakfast and, without another word about her being a princess or a siren, they'd taken off driving across land that was all but empty. She wondered where they were, but decided silence was her best choice at the moment.

"Did you find anything in your research, O wise one?" Bianca asked Loch from the back seat where she and Seamus sat. Gwen bit her lips to keep from smiling, instead keeping her gaze focused on the landscape outside the window.

"I'm waiting to hear back from a few contacts. But, from what I gathered, half-sirens, especially of royal fae blood, are highly unusual. I'm not sure what that means; however, because Gwen was gifted the bracelets, I can at least make the assumption that she was welcomed by the fae side of her family. Had she been shunned, she would never have received such a gift."

Gwen glanced down at her magickal bracelets, seeing them in a new light. They were a connection to her family – a sign of acceptance and love. Even though she hadn't ever felt uncared for or unloved, it was still nice to know that she had additional support from her unknown family.

"And the siren side of my family?" Gwen asked, glancing at Loch. Today he had donned his leathers again, making Gwen's mouth all but water when she looked at him. Too bad he wasn't for her – if a girl was going to test the waters, he'd be the one to do it with. Although, to be fair, she wasn't sure that dipping her toe in that pond would be the smartest move for her. Siren or not, she was inexperienced, and a man like Loch would probably not tolerate her fumbling attempts. He seemed more like the type who liked to take charge, or meet his woman head-on while she carried a whip or something. Rolling her eyes at her active imagination, Gwen shook her head and focused back on the landscape rolling past the window.

"It's an unknown, this siren side. The fae don't necessarily clash with sirens, but they also don't particularly associate with them either. Apparently both groups, by tacit agreement, decided to give each other a wide berth. I think sirens have considerable strength and magick, yet I'm at a loss to tell you how their society is organized or what their typical mating rituals are and so on. It's fascinating to me that one of our royals took up with one – even I would know better than to do so."

And there it was, Gwen thought, feeling inexplicably miffed at his words. Granted, she would probably advise anyone to stay away from a siren as well. But now these were her people and she was half-siren, so it bothered her.

"Right, right. Wouldn't want to be caught slumming with us lowlifes," Gwen said dryly, taking a sip from the water flask she carried in her lap to wet the lump in her throat.

"Your race is an unknown. Sure, myths and legends abound, but in all reality you're untested magick. It's best not to rock the boat, to keep separate – which allows both societies to live in peace," Loch said carefully.

"Live and let live?" Bianca asked.

"Precisely. It's neither good nor bad; it just is."

"So truly, the unknown here is my mother. The siren herself," Gwen said carefully, testing the words out. Her mother. That had been something she'd just resigned herself to not knowing much about. And once she had come to that decision, she'd made her peace with it.

"Certainly. There must be a reason she gave you up – perhaps you couldn't live in the water as they do, being a half-blood," Loch mused.

Gwen tried to not let the term 'half-blood' bother her. It just sounded a bit derogatory, was all.

"I mean, would they kill their young? Or young that weren't pure? Wait a minute – aren't all sirens women? So how do they reproduce? And they would have to keep some of their young, right?" Bianca mused.

Gwen turned around to raise an eyebrow at her.

"That's actually a very interesting point. How do sirens carry on their race? And if there are no men, how are they reproducing?" Gwen thought about it, then thought about a society of male sirens, which made her giggle. "Can you imagine male sirens? They'd be singing to the women on the shore and the women would be like, 'nah, we're good.'"

"But we have pizza and video games," Bianca quipped, and she and Gwen burst into laughter.

"And hairy chests," Seamus added, cracking them up even more.

"Though I'd probably get sucked in by pizza and video games, I'm not going to lie," Gwen admitted, and Seamus immediately began peppering her with questions about her favorite video games. An hour passed, and she soon realized they were drawing closer to the coast. Though she'd be hard pressed to explain how she knew, she could feel it in her bones – they were near water. Perhaps it had come as her birthright.

"Where are we?" Gwen asked, turning to look at Loch.

"Along the west coast. I've heard tell of sirens along these waters, so I figured we might as well head this way. Unless you have a better idea or a clue?"

"Just the clue that came with the bracelets."

Bianca tapped Gwen's shoulder and said in a loud whisper, "That would have been a helpful bit of knowledge to have."

"Right, right. Sorry about that." Gwen flushed, and dug the paper from a pocket in her purse. "Fire and Ice, Song by Song, Day by Night, One follows along."

"Ohhh, beautiful," Bianca breathed.

"I think we can surmise 'song by song' is a siren-related thing," Seamus said.

"As is probably the 'one follows along.' Follow the siren's song," Bianca mused.

Gwen held up her wrists so that the cuffs showed.

"Fire and ice?"

"No. Past the Aran Islands I've heard tell of a spot on an island which both spits molten lava and boasts a waterfall of ice. Nobody knows quite where it is located," Loch said.

"But you do?"

"Aye, I'm thinking it's far past the Aran Islands."

"Do you think it's a metaphor for the two races? Fire for fae and ice for the sirens? Merged together as one?" Gwen asked, and the car went silent.

"That's... not a bad thought. I think we need to get ourselves a boat," Loch said.

"Can't we just take the ferry to the islands?" Bianca asked.

"And risk killing Domnua in front of tourists? You have to know they are going to try for us whenever we're vulnerable," Loch pointed out, pulling out his cell phone to punch in a number one-handed. He spoke in a language Gwen didn't recognize, and was off the phone in a matter of moments.

"All good. Ladies, I hope you have your sea legs. It's going to be a rough passage."

Loch wasn't lying, Gwen thought as they rolled up to a small bay tucked behind some foreboding hills a while later. Though she'd been dying to use her phone to look up more information on the sirens, Bianca had forbidden her to do so. Something about the bad fae being able to track electronics easily. It annoyed her, but she accepted it. The last thing Gwen wanted to do was invite more trouble on this quest.

"That's your boat, I'm assuming?" Bianca asked, pointing to where a yacht was moored to a small dock, the waves careening into the shore and crashing against its shiny red hull.

"Yes," Loch answered, pulling the car to a stop.

"Nice. You know how to drive this thing?" Gwen asked as they all got out and began to unpack the SUV.

"Yes," Loch said again, this time with a huge sigh.

"Oooookay," Gwen all but snarled at him, but then forced her temper down. She was a happy person – anger never got her anywhere, nor would it do so now. Channeling her inner zen, she helped bring bags and packs from the SUV over to the dock, though nobody set foot on the boat yet. In moments, her anger had dissipated and she was back to her happy mood.

So happy, in fact, that she forgot herself and began to sing gently under her breath, her face lifted to the breeze tearing along the rocky shoreline, enjoying the light mist in the air. It wasn't a perfect spring day, but Gwen so loved the sea in all of its moods.

"Gwen! No!"

Gwen snapped back to attention, whirling in time to see a wave of Domnua flood over the hills, this time on horses, crossbows at the ready and arrows already launching through the air. She had but a moment to draw a deep breath before she was plucked from the ground and cradled in Loch's arms, his large shoulders protecting her as he dodged arrow after arrow, pirouetting as neatly as a ballet dancer and dodging like a football player. In seconds, she'd been deposited in a berth belowdecks with nothing more than a curt order to stay put.

"Like hell I will," Gwen said, staring at the door as faint shouts reached her from outside. Standing, she grabbed the door and tugged. Once, twice, and then a third time. Realizing she was locked in, Gwen swore loudly and drew her bracelets back to throw ice at the lock, not caring what kind of damage she might do to the boat – and screamed in frustration when the ice met an impenetrable barrier of magick and shattered to pieces at her feet.

Furious, Gwen flopped on the bed and waited. She prayed her careless actions wouldn't cost anyone's life.

CHAPTER 19

"*I*'m sorry," Gwen said, jumping up from the bed as soon as the door opened. Loch stood there, his huge frame filling the narrow door, his chest still heaving with exhaustion from the fight. "Is everyone safe?"

"Aye, we're safe," Loch said, his eyes still on hers before he turned and walked away. "No thanks to you."

Shame filled Gwen. He was right, though he didn't have to be so nasty about it. But she hadn't been the one who had to fight the battle. Trudging after him down the narrow hallway, she climbed the ladder to find Seamus and Bianca loading the supplies that had survived onto the boat.

"I'm sorry," Gwen said, rushing over to take a box from Bianca, nervous her new friend would be angry with her.

"For what? I'm just glad you were safe. One less thing to worry about," Bianca said, shooting Gwen an easy smile as she took Seamus's hand and hopped on the boat.

"For singing. I wasn't thinking. I was just in a good mood and I started singing sort of under my breath like I usually do, and… well, they appeared," Gwen said, knowing her face had to be flaming red in embarrassment.

"You need to think more," Loch said, lifting several of the boxes in one arm and swinging down below to store them.

"I…" Gwen stopped herself from shouting after him, guilt still making her stomach turn.

"Don't listen to him. He's just a big grump. The Domnua can and will come at any moment. Whether you sing or not. They're hunting us, and we're well aware of what we have ourselves involved in," Seamus said, throwing an arm over Gwen's shoulder to give her a loose squeeze. "It's not on you that they attacked us. It's on the Domnua. Remember that."

"It really isn't," Bianca added. "Don't let Loch bully you. He's just doing that because he was scared he wouldn't get to you in time. You know how men get when they want to protect their women," she said, then laughed in delight at the look on Loch's face as he heard her words.

"I'm not his woman," Gwen protested.

"She's not my woman," Loch agreed, shooting Gwen a glare. "I'm simply pointing out the fact that she should know better than to sing – especially if it is one of the things that can quite literally draw evil to us. You'd think she'd pay more attention."

"It was a mistake. An honest one, at that," Gwen said, squaring off with Loch so that they were face to face. Well, they would have been, except for him being so tall she had to lean back to look up at him.

"We don't have room for mistakes. Not if you want us to protect you and help you find your treasure," Loch said, his eyes all but glowing with anger.

"I never asked for you to protect me," Gwen hissed, and surprised Loch by poking him in the chest with her finger.

She wasn't surprised to be met with a wall of muscle, as she'd felt it when he'd cradled her to his chest earlier.

"I never asked to protect you. It's a punishment, okay?" Loch almost shouted. Gwen inadvertently took a step back, even more upset than before. "I couldn't care less about this stupid quest, aside from the fact that it allows me to kill Domnua, which I delight in doing. But protecting you? Yeah, it's nothing but a punishment for me. So get that straight the next time you want to do something so stupid as singing down a mountain of Domnua on your head and almost getting killed on the spot. Some of us are here because of our duty and nothing else. You have no right to put our lives on the line."

Gwen felt like the air had been sucked out of her in one big whoosh. She was left gasping when Loch stormed off, throwing off the bow lines himself and firing up the engine. They pulled away from the dock as quickly as the yacht could move, putting distance between themselves and the land where Domnua might still roam. Gwen turned to move to the front of the boat, her hands clutching the railing as she looked blindly out over the rough waves, not caring about the salty spray hitting her face.

"Here," Bianca said, nudging Gwen and holding out a steaming cup of what turned out to be tea spiked with whiskey.

"Thanks," Gwen said, carefully taking the cup. She braced herself against the railing so she could hold on with one hand and still sip the tea without falling over.

"Don't let him get to you," Bianca said, but Gwen shook her head, stopping her friend.

"He's right, though. I was careless. And I have no right to be putting any of you in danger, whether you're here for punishment or a job or whatever. I should really just go my own way and figure this out alone. It's not fair to any of you," Gwen said, her eyes still out on the horizon, feeling deflated.

"Sounds like you're having a bit of a pity party. Not on my watch," Bianca said sternly, and Gwen turned and raised an eyebrow at her. "Here's the deal, sweets. Seamus and I? We're in this. Period. We know the risks, and we've been in a lot of battles over the past few months. But this is about more than just us. We're fighting for the good – for life as we know it. For all the people out there who don't even know they're in danger. Babies being born, lovers getting married, grandmothers having tea with their knitting circles. It's about more than just you or me or even Loch and his people. And guess what? You didn't sign up for this either. It was assigned to you. It could be viewed as a punishment for you, too. And yet you embraced it as a challenge and have smiled cheerfully in the face of danger. Now is not the time for a pity party, my friend. Not in the slightest."

Gwen smiled and bumped Bianca's shoulder with her own, feeling the truth of her words settle over her shoulders. Taking a sip of whiskey, she let the warmth fill her as the salty spray continued to buffet them in the face.

"Thanks. You're good for me, my friend," Gwen said.

"Don't let Loch get to you. Seriously. He's just shaken up because you were surrounded and he was worried he wouldn't get to you in time. Did you see how he cradled you in his arms to protect you from the arrows? Swoon," Bianca gushed, making Gwen laugh.

"He's quite strong," Gwen agreed. "Though he put some spell on the door to keep me from getting out of the berth below. It really made me angry – all I could do was listen to the sounds of the battle and not help."

"See? He just wanted to keep you safe. You can't fault him for that. He's not used to discussing his feelings, is all. But don't let him off too easy, girl. Men like him aren't used to apologizing. He needs to grovel a bit," Bianca assured her, tapping the rim of her glass against Gwen's.

"Oh, he doesn't need to apologize. It's not a big deal. Really. And I don't think he has feelings. Trust me, it's not like that," Gwen protested.

"I know what I see. But... as Seamus says, I can be a bit of a meddler. I'll just be letting this one run its course. Now, I'm ready to get in, out of this spray and wind. What about you?"

"I'm going to finish my tea out here and then I'll be in," Gwen said, then reached out impulsively to hug her friend. "Thanks for the talk. I needed it. I'm feeling more sorted out now."

"That's what I'm here for!"

CHAPTER 20

*G*wen kept quiet through the dinner preparations and the meal, offering her help whenever she could. It took most of her willpower to ignore Loch, as she wasn't one to hold a grudge, but somehow she managed to do so. When Bianca and Seamus both looked weary on their feet, Loch instructed them to go to bed, and promised to wake Seamus at four o'clock to switch watch. From what Gwen understood, it was to be a longer crossing than she had expected, largely due to the swells making the boat rock back and forth, slowing their progress.

Still feeling guilty from earlier – though intellectually she understood that she didn't need to – Gwen decided to deliver a cup of coffee to Loch on the bridge.

"Coffee," Gwen said, infusing some niceness into her voice. It just wasn't in her to be petty or angry, though Loch probably deserved her being cold to him.

Loch glanced over at her from where he stood, arms crossed on his chest, eyes trained on the digital instruments in front of him.

"Appreciate it," Loch finally said, reaching out and taking the cup from her. Gwen tried to ignore the little tingle of electricity that seemed to jump from him to her when his fingers brushed over hers. Silence stretched out before them, and Gwen settled in to wait, knowing that eventually he'd talk. It always amused her when people didn't seem to understand that silence was an excellent tool in negotiations. And right now, she wanted to know what this punishment of Loch's was all about. Taking a seat in the captain's chair – which Loch had eschewed to stand, glowering, at the window – she crossed her legs and stared at the dark windows. Nothing but the glow from the bow lights showed against the water.

"I'm sorry," Loch finally said, startling Gwen from her daydream about mermaids and sirens. The words sounded unused against his lips, which made them even more meaningful to Gwen. Deciding to be kind, she shrugged a shoulder even though he wasn't looking at her.

"I'm getting used to your outbursts now. Don't think anything of it," Gwen said cheerfully.

"Outbursts? I don't have outbursts," Loch said, slanting a glance at her in the cozy light of the room.

"As I'm the one on the receiving end of most of them, I'd be saying they're outbursts," Gwen said easily.

"Perhaps the last one might be considered more expressive than I usually am," Loch admitted.

Gwen was delighted to see a wry smile cross his face. If the man was handsome when he glowered at her, he was devastating when he smiled. He was going to make some fairy princess quite happy someday.

"Care to tell me about this punishment that's been inflicted upon you?" Gwen asked, deciding they were back on somewhat equal ground now.

"Not in the slightest," Loch said, but his tone held less bite. He straightened and adjusted something on the screen and Gwen felt a subtle shift in the boat.

"That's fine. I've a great imagination. I read a lot of comic books and fantasy stories. Let me think…" Gwen drummed her fingers on her lips and then snapped them. "You were meant to save a princess from drinking a potion that would turn her into a dragon. You didn't get there in time and she slaughtered a whole village with her fiery wrath."

Loch cast a 'you must be crazy' look at her and shook his head, but she saw his lips twitch. Encouraged, she tried again.

"No? Okay, um, let's see. Tiny garden gnomes came to life and took their years of angst about people stealing from their gardens out on the village. A bloodbath ensued, with the gnomes ultimately using the blood of the dead to harvest the best crop of vegetables they'd had in a hundred years."

At that Loch turned, both eyebrows raised.

"You're a bloodthirsty woman, aren't you?"

"Not particularly. Just a healthy imagination." Gwen laughed at herself. "Plus, I figured it was something dramatic and blood-ridden to get a sorcerer like you punished. But maybe I'm embellishing. I suppose I don't know anything that isn't myths about the fae. I imagine everything in your world is fairly dramatic and magickal."

"It's certainly not as dull as human life seems to be. And yet we find ourselves drawn to humans all the time. We love watching the resilience of the human spirit, their often-fool-hardy fearlessness, and their headlong slides into love. Aye, the fae world has its magick, but so does the human world."

Gwen realized that was the nicest thing he had said yet about humans. Warming to him, she smiled brightly in his direction, surprised when he returned it with a smile of his own.

"That's nice of you to say, at least about us lowly mortal beings. Well, perhaps the most poetic. You are a man of few words, Loch. Except when you're yelling at me," Gwen said, relaxing back into the chair, the rolling of the boat lulling her.

"You aren't human, Gwen. You shouldn't be forgetting that."

That sent a shiver of excitement through her.

"I'm still getting used to that concept. I've lived my life as a full human until about a month ago when I stumbled upon my ice power. So forgive me if I identify as one."

"That's fair. Though it would be fun to see you dressed as a fairy princess, reveling in your power over the peasants below you."

"I would be nothing if not benevolent in my ruling." When Gwen laughed, Loch did as well, tension seeming to fall away from him as he leaned back to study her.

"I'm certain you would. My people would like you."

"Can you tell me about them? My… family, I suppose?"

"I can. Even better, I'll take you there when this is all over. We've got to go get your gran anyhow," Loch said. "But I can tell you that the fae are an endlessly interesting people. We like to excel at all things, we love riddles and games, and we relish all the things that bring us pleasure – from shiny, sparkly jewelry and luscious silks to the pleasures of the flesh. We're an organized society, one that defaults to following our court of royals, and rare it is for a fae to break the laws. Especially the most ancient and deadly of laws." Loch muttered the last bit almost under his breath and Gwen tilted her head at him, pulling her mind away from images of fae cavorting in silk and making love under the stars.

"Which is what you did, isn't it? You broke a sacred law."

Loch paused for a moment, his eyes back on the dark windows, his face drawn, before he nodded once.

"Aye."

"Well, you had to have done it for a good reason. You wouldn't have just broken it for fun or greed," Gwen said automatically, surprising Loch into looking at her.

"How could you possibly know that?"

"I just know. Sure, you're crass and rough around the edges and more often cranky than not, but you're also altruistic and honor-bound and ultimately, you show up when you're needed. Even if you don't want to be here, you don't shirk your duty. No, something had to have forced your hand into breaking the law," Gwen concluded, feeling a little breathless at the way his eyes stared at her while she talked, dropping once to her lips, before meeting hers again with such intensity that she felt a little lightheaded.

"Don't get ideas about me, Princess Gwen. I'm not a good man," Loch finally said, after a long moment.

"Ideas? I have no ideas about you other than I'm certain you wouldn't break a sacred law unless absolutely necessary," Gwen said, feeling miffed that he was turning this story into something more.

"I can see the way you look at me," Loch said, "I can tell when a woman has… ideas."

Gwen's mouth dropped open in surprise as she looked at him, taking in the almost smug look on his handsome face before she burst into laughter.

"Men like you don't go for women like me," she said, her body convulsing in laughter. "Though I suppose you are used to women falling all over you, I'm well aware that I'm not the woman for you. But you're quite handsome. I can see the appeal. I'm certain you have no trouble finding yourself a woman."

Loch looked a little disgruntled at that, and Gwen sighed.

"I'm sorry if you were thinking there was more here or that I had a crush... it's not like that. I just have an honest admiration for your sheer male beauty, but I'm well aware that I'm not your type."

"Beauty?" Loch now looked disgusted. "And who says you aren't my type? Why wouldn't you be my type?"

Gwen pointed down to her baggy cardigan and loose pants.

"I'm a geek, I don't wear flowing gowns or glitzy rings, and I'm certainly not an accomplished mistress. You probably go for, like, the Salma Hayek or Charlize Theron types. Badass women who have their way with men."

"And you think you aren't a badass woman? I saw you mow down about a billion Domnua yesterday without blinking an eye," Loch countered.

"Well, sure, I suppose badass like that. But not... er..." Gwen was about to say 'in the bedroom,' then blushed, glad that the soft glow from the bridge would hopefully mask the flush on her face.

"But not... where? In bed? As a lover? Are you timid then, sweet Gwen of the Sirens?" Loch laughed, then paused as he studied her face more closely. Gwen found herself blushing even more furiously, and deliberately turned her chin away so she didn't meet his eyes.

She didn't even hear him move. One moment he was on the other side of the bridge and the next he stood right in front of her, his arms on either side of the chair, locking her in place as he brought his face inches away from hers.

"Have you never been with a man?" Loch asked, surprise

coating his every word, and embarrassment worked its way through Gwen.

"Of course I have. I was just raised that it isn't polite to discuss... that... in company," Gwen scoffed, her eyes still averted.

"Methinks you are lying," Loch said, his breath whispering lightly over her face, bringing every nerve ending in her body to attention.

"I have! You're just trying to intimidate me. I know how to be with a man," Gwen said, exasperated and feeling annoyed about him cornering her in the chair. Deciding to put him off his game, she reached up and grabbed his face, pulling his lips to hers in a kiss.

Heat coursed between them, instantly awakening her, and she held still, her lips pressed to his and her eyes closed, unsure of what to do next. Her body was telling her one thing, but in all reality, she felt awkward and uncertain about anything to do with kissing or sex in general. Aside from a few sloppy kisses in school, she really had no experience with men.

Loch pulled back, his face still inches from hers, and met her eyes.

"See?" Gwen said, "I know what I'm doing. I'm just saying that I'm not your type, and we can both admit there is no chemistry here. I'm for bed then." She stood and slipped beneath his arm to make a quick escape, her cheeks burning with embarrassment.

The breath rushed out of her when Loch whirled her to him, pressing her body fully against his length, his lips claiming hers in a kiss so powerful she felt it down to her toes. Frozen, unable to think, she squeaked while he explored her lips with his own, gently nibbling them until he urged them lightly apart to touch his tongue to hers. Gwen shuddered against him, pleasure careening through her as he explored her mouth, his kiss a quest, a promise of something so much deeper, and yet delivering so much pleasure on its own. When she moaned against his mouth, he pulled back, raking one hand through his hair.

"I'd say there's chemistry here," Loch said, not seeming to be entirely pleased by the thought.

Gwen gulped, unsure of how to respond or what to say. So in true geek fashion, she fled the bridge, letting the door slam behind her and the cool wind slap her in the face.

Touching her lips, she found them curved in a smile.

CHAPTER 21

*L*och's hands gripped the wheel. He needed something to hold onto. Everything in his gut screamed for him to go after this woman – Gwen of the Sirens. His mind flashed to her in the shower, lush curves begging for his touch, her red curls tumbling around her body. His body ached for release as he thought about burying himself deep inside her and showing her the pleasures of the flesh.

Aye, that was one thing he was certain of – Gwen was untouched. The thought of another man touching her, taking her innocence, made him want to rage.

Loch thought about earlier today, when she'd been casually walking on the beach, a small smile on her lips, her face turned to the sky. He admired so much about the way she handled things, to the point that he was almost a little jealous of it. No matter what, she seemed to look for – and find – the good in any situation or person. Here they were, loading a boat on a drizzly gray day and she had still looked to the sky and sung a song. It was the type of optimism that made his heart clench in his chest.

When the Domnua had poured over the hills, he'd panicked for a moment – and in that moment, he'd frozen. Luckily, his training had jarred him into motion, though it had taken his brain a few moments to catch up before he could start working protection magick to surround her. But in those few moments, seeing the arrows landing so close to where she stood, he'd come to a very serious conclusion.

Gwenith, the fairy siren, was his mate.

He'd known when he'd heard her sing, but hadn't been ready to accept it. But her very presence in his space drew him. She was like a magnet and he was pulled inexplicably to her force.

The problem was, he didn't like it.

Loch had bigger plans for his life, none of which included him settling down with anyone long-term. He had watched as other fae had partnered up, watched as they had compromised on their choices in life, and he wasn't willing to do so. As a sorcerer, Loch had a higher calling – to serve his people and the royal fae above him.

No, he didn't have the time or inclination for a partner in his life, so it would be best if he kept Gwen at a distance. No matter how much he itched to hold her, to touch her, even to make her laugh, it was not to be.

He'd protect her and see this quest through. But after that, he'd knock any stars out of her eyes.

And move on alone, as he was destined to be.

CHAPTER 22

*G*wen couldn't help herself. She slipped to the bow of the boat, her body still thrumming with the intensity of the kiss. It was her first real kiss, and it shamed her to realize that, even to herself. Though she shouldn't feel shame, Gwen lectured herself as she leaned against the railing; Gran had often reminded her that many women were late bloomers.

Oh! But to be kissed by a man who knew what he was doing and not some fumbling schoolboy. Gwen grinned and pressed her hand to her lips again, tracing them and doing her best to commit the sensations to memory. No matter what happened, she'd have this moment in time – a passionate kiss on a boat to a magickal island after a fierce battle. She supposed as first-real-kiss stories went, it was pretty damn good.

Gwen wondered what he was thinking about her. Did he have feelings for her? Or was this just his way of having fun and passing time? She'd been warned about men who stole kisses from all the girls. They had a different woman every night of the week and not a speck of honor. It didn't seem likely that Loch was a man like that, but she was certain he'd had many lovers in his past. Would he be the type to love and walk away? Or would he have long-term relationships with women – no, fae? Gwen couldn't see him as the boyfriend type. He struck her more as a lone wolf than anything. Even traveling with this group seemed to make him antsy and she remembered how surprised he seemed every time one of them jumped in to help.

"Just lovers he's had then," Gwen muttered, staring down into the blue water where the light illuminated the depths. "But not love. Not really. I can't think a man like him would give love easily."

She watched the waves slap the hull, delighting in the way they seemed to curl and dance, almost mesmerized by the beauty of the water. It had always been this way for her around water. It called to her, soothed her, entranced her. Perhaps that was why she'd begun playing with the ice concept, she mused, staring dreamily at the water, the sky dark above her with low cloud cover.

When the water reached up and pulled her in, Gwen barely had time to squeak before she was plunged into the freezing waters of the Atlantic and pulled beneath the boat, her head narrowly missing the blades of the propeller as she was dragged down into darkness. Invisible hands bound hers, keeping her from swimming, and Gwen watched the light of the boat sail away as she was forced into the depths toward her inevitable death.

CHAPTER 23

*H*e'd been watching her on the deck camera. Loch would have been embarrassed to admit it if it hadn't signaled to him that she'd gone over the edge. In seconds he had the engine off and was stripping his boots, his shouts of alarm rousing Seamus and Bianca.

"What's going on?" Bianca raced onto the deck, followed by Seamus, both pulling sweaters over their heads.

"She went over. Man the helm. They've taken her into the ocean," Loch shouted, then went straight over the railing into the dark water, barely flinching as the icy water shocked his system. Instead, his mind raced to run as much magick as he could, starting first with the spell that let him breathe underwater. It was something he'd been working on for a while, and as of yet he'd not taught it to any of the other fae. It would last him but minutes before the spell wore off, which was why he needed to perfect it before he revealed it to his brethren.

Slanting his eyelids slightly open, he spied a dull glow and sped as fast as he could through the water, his fingers becoming webbed as he furiously worked magick after magick to drive himself closer to where he could feel Gwen was.

Impossibly deep.

His heart thudded in his chest as he raced closer and, sending out his magick, he began to try and pick off anything he felt was bad energy around where he could sense Gwen's heart pulsing. Loch's mind raced furiously as he worked to fend off the Domnua and also send Gwen pockets of air so she could breathe – anything to keep her alive, just until he could get there.

But he feared it was too late. They'd been down too long, and too far. He felt a scream building inside him as he worked nearer to where she was, seeing the dull light of her magick begin to fade, the icy water crushing her life spirit to darkness.

Something flitted past him, so fast he barely caught the movement before more mirrored it, the power of their motion pulling Loch along like he was caught in a riptide. He had but a moment to fear for his own life before he realized what was happening.

The sirens had come to save their own.

CHAPTER 24

*I*nexplicably, Gwen stopped feeling afraid. The closer she slipped toward death, the less scared she seemed to feel. Here, in the darkness of the icy water, she found that she could still take little sips of air, as if she was absorbing bubbles of air from the water itself. Was she filtering the water into oxygen? She realized that she must be nearing death – if she was calmly contemplating how she was breathing and not all that concerned about the Domnua still pulling her deeper into the water, then certainly she'd accepted her fate.

How silly of her to let her guard down, Gwen thought, then twisted when she felt the bonds holding her hands tight to her body break. That was interesting. Had she lost the Domnua? Stretching her arms out, she gasped, choking back water that did enter her mouth this time, shocking her into realizing she was still very much alive and this wasn't a dream. Arms looped through hers, carrying her briskly higher and higher toward, she presumed, the surface.

It was strange; in this darkly cold water, she couldn't

visually tell what was up or what was down, but her gut told her they were heading toward the surface. It was the 'they' part of the equation that was tripping her up. Who had her arms and was saving her – rocketing her at a speed far past safety for her to surface?

When they broke the surface, Gwen gasped for air, her lungs screaming in pain, dots playing across her eyes as she was held above the waves that threatened to crash into her face again. Looking around, her gaze met eyes of a similar color to her own.

Gwen froze.

There in the water, glowing faintly with otherworldly magick, were what she presumed to be sirens. Or mermaids. Perhaps both? With almost translucent skin the color of moon-light and luminous blue eyes, they swam around her, singing and singing, songs of such joy and such calm that Gwen was immediately warmed from within. No longer did the cold touch her, no longer did her body gasp for air. They were healing her with their song and Gwen never wanted them to leave.

When Loch broke the surface next to her, his eyes wild, the song reached a crescendo of such joy it was as though the ocean thundered with it. He wrapped his arms around her, holding her to his chest so that her head stayed above water. Gwen closed her eyes for a moment, blissfully, almost mind-lessly content to have his arms wrapped around her, knowing that in this one moment everything would be just fine.

Her heart pounded in her chest as, one by one, the mermaids began to swim away. Gwen didn't want them to leave yet. She had questions – she needed them to stay.

"Wait," she croaked, beginning to shiver as they took their warmth with them.

"Shh, save your energy, my child." The last mermaid, a woman of unusual beauty, pressed her lips to Gwen's, blowing air straight into her lungs and sending the breath of life – of love – through her until she was warm straight through to her toes. "Know that you are loved. We'll fight this battle with you. The fae from land, and the sirens from the depths. Have no fear of the water. We'll always be here for you."

With one more gentle kiss, the siren disappeared, forever changing Gwen's definition of family, of beauty, and reshaping her understanding of the world. When a life ring splashed by her head, she realized they had been delivered back to the yacht.

"Are you okay? Did they hurt you?" Gwen asked Loch as they both hooked an arm to the ring. They were pulled to the swim platform at the back of the boat, where a terrified-looking Bianca stood, her arms wrapped around her body as she rocked back and forth.

"A bit chilly, but I'll make it," Loch grumbled against her neck. "Friends of yours?"

Gwen found herself laughing, turning so that her forehead bumped his, though she refrained from kissing him like she found herself desperately wanting to do.

"It seems so."

"Good friends to have, I'd say. I wasn't sure I'd reach you in time." Loch scrambled onto the swim platform and pulled her easily from the water, reminding her once again of his great strength.

"What happened?! Were those mermaids? Oh my god, I honestly thought you both were gone. We couldn't see you. It was so dark and you both were just gone. We had nothing to go on," Bianca chattered away, dancing from foot to foot in her fright, until Gwen reached out to pat her arm.

"I'm okay. But I'd dearly love to get out of these wet clothes. It's a mite bit cold out here, no?"

Glad to be tasked with something, Bianca all but dragged Gwen inside to the kitchen quarters, where Gwen soon found herself divested of her wet clothes and wrapped in heavy woolen blankets, a cup of hot tea steaming in her hands.

"It's amazing how tea is always the answer for anything," Gwen mused. She took a sip to find another bracing shot of whiskey in the mug. Bianca only shrugged when Gwen tilted her head at her.

"If you can't be enjoying a tipple of whiskey after a moment like that, then I'm not certain what's the point of having whiskey around anyway," Bianca pointed out.

Gwen nodded her agreement. "Cheers then," she said, and smiled when Seamus and Loch clambered down the stairs – Loch in flannel pants and a sweater, and Seamus grinning when he saw Gwen's face.

"It's pleased I am to be seeing the color back in your cheeks. You were frightfully pale when you came up from the water," Seamus said, pressing a quick kiss to her cheek before moving to snuggle up next to Bianca.

"Thank you," Gwen said, her gaze on Loch as he sat across from her at the table – close, but far enough away that they weren't touching. She wondered if that was intentional or not.

"You're welcome, of course. I couldn't let you go down without a fight," Loch said, then picked up the whiskey and took a long pull right from the bottle.

"What happened?" Bianca demanded.

"I… I don't really know. I was at the bow just looking

into the water and it was like the waves reached up and pulled me under. I couldn't do anything – I was quite literally bound. I think the Domnua had my arms pulled behind my back. I couldn't move at all – couldn't bring my bracelets up, nothing. And they were so fast! I swear I was down fifty meters in a second," Gwen said, shaking her head in disbelief.

"That is terrifying." Bianca shuddered and Seamus rubbed her back. "How did you not die though? I mean, is it because you're part siren? Can you breathe underwater?"

"I don't really know, to be honest. It was like I was able to inhale these little pockets of air or something. I can't say. I've never really tried to breathe underwater before. I always assumed I couldn't, so I've held my breath anytime I've gone swimming."

"I may have helped with that," Loch said, and explained about one of the spells he had been sending to her.

"Good thinking, especially in a stressful situation like that. Were you able to do the same for yourself?" Seamus asked, and the two men launched into a discussion of spells. Loch looked animated for the first time in a while as he explained some of the thought processes behind the magicks he'd been working on.

Incredibly, Gwen felt her eyes beginning to close.

"So... what happened then? Like, how did you get rid of the Domnua?" Bianca asked, pulling Gwen back to reality before she dozed off.

"My family. The mermaids. They saved me," Gwen said, mumbling a bit. Now that her adrenaline had spiked, she was crashing, and crashing hard.

"Mermaids! I want every detail," Bianca began, but then she saw Gwen's droopy eyes. "Tomorrow, that is. You've had quite the ordeal. Loch, can you carry her to bed?"

Gwen wanted to protest, but found she had no strength to do so. She needed to be prone and out – now. She meekly said her goodnights as Loch cradled her to his chest, his warmth enveloping her as he took her to her tiny cabin. He stretched her out on the bed, and Gwen moaned in pleasure at the comfort of the small bunk and the warmth of the blankets. Feeling cocooned in safety and warmth, she smiled up at Loch.

"Thank you," Gwen whispered, her eyes closed.

Silence answered her.

But she felt the whisper of a kiss – so light it was like a butterfly had breezed past – before the door to her cabin closed.

Gwen smiled as she slipped into sleep.

CHAPTER 25

*I*t was as though she'd been in a coma, she'd slept so deeply, Gwen thought as she blinked awake and rolled to stare at the clock. She wondered briefly if Loch had worked some sort of magick spell for her to sleep so soundly or if it had been the shock of the whole experience that had knocked her out.

Gwen stretched and pulled the blanket around her, knowing she would need to get up soon to pull her weight, but wanting a moment to snuggle into her warm cocoon of blankets and relive the events that had transpired.

And to think she'd been content with her day-to-day life when there was so much magick in the world.

Gwen almost squealed in delight when she thought about all the spells that Loch could do – something she didn't yet understand but planned to grill him on at some point. She couldn't even bring herself to fully unpack the awesomeness of seeing the mermaids without filling in Bianca about it as well. Her stomach growled, reminding her that she hadn't eaten in god knew how long, and Gwen jumped up to leave the bunk just as the door opened.

Seeing Loch's mouth drop open as he stared at her reminded Gwen that she'd been divested of her sopping wet and torn clothes the night before. Which meant she once again stood before him naked. This time, she cocked a hand on her hip and glared at him.

"Have you ever heard of the concept of knocking before?" Gwen scolded.

Loch had the decency to blush. "I'm sorry," he said, but he didn't leave. His eyes drank her in and Gwen felt the mood in the room begin to shift, like an undercurrent of energy that seemed to pulse between the two of them.

"And yet… you're still here," Gwen pointed out, her mouth having gone dry.

"I… I just… You're stunning." Loch swallowed and then ducked out the door, slamming it behind him. She wouldn't have been surprised if he'd locked her in the room once more, simply to keep himself out.

For the first time ever, Gwen began to feel a thrill of feminine power. Even if she found it hard to believe that Loch would find her 'stunning,' she realized he was kind enough to compliment her, seeing as she was standing naked in front of him.

But still… there had been something there.

Remembering the kiss from last night, Gwen traced her fingers over her lips once more before pulling a blanket around her and cracking the door to poke her head out. A pile of clothes sat in front of the door on the floor of the small hallway and Gwen snatched them up, grateful that she wouldn't have to walk around all day in a blanket.

Happy to see that her pants had made it, she pulled them

on, but scowled at the rest of the clothes. A shell pink long-sleeved scoop neck shirt and a fleece jacket were the options. No bra, and no Star Wars shirt or cardigan to be found. Sighing, she pulled the pink shirt over her head and glared down at where it hugged her breasts. She could only imagine what a sight that was with no bra on. Still, it was better than a blanket, she reminded herself. Picking up the coat, she made her way to the toilet before venturing to the galley to sniff out something to eat.

Bianca whistled her appreciation when Gwen walked in. Loch turned from where he was preparing tea, dropping the packet on the floor when he caught sight of her. With a curse, he picked it up and all but fled from the kitchen.

"Bad?" Gwen asked, grateful to see a tray of toast on the small table.

"Amazing," Bianca said, casting an eye over the shirt and whistling once more. "Girl, I did not see the curves you had hiding under all those baggy clothes, but hot damn. Loch doesn't stand a chance. Plus the pink goes great with your red hair."

"It's not a color I normally wear," Gwen admitted, trying not to gobble down the piece of toast in one bite to calm the growling in her stomach.

"You should. But wow, we may need to find you a bra or keep your coat zipped up. I'm thinking even Seamus will be distracted."

Immediately feeling guilty, Gwen pulled the fleece jacket on. Though it was fitted as well, it at least provided another layer of coverage.

"I'm sorry. It was the only option. I wasn't trying to, you know, show anything off."

"Trust me, I know. You should show it off. All the time. If

I looked like you, I certainly would," Bianca said, cheerful as ever.

"But you're beautiful," Gwen protested.

"I'm cute. Maybe even pretty. But not a knockout like you. And I'm okay with that. I've got a man who loves me and an awesome life. I know Seamus and I are meant for each other. Besides, you've not a man-stealing bone in your body. You're pure heart, you are. I've not a worry over you. Plus, no man will try for you so long as Loch is in the picture," Bianca said, putting jam on a piece of toast.

"He kissed me," Gwen blurted, and then flushed. "Well, I kissed him. Then he kissed me back. And... I don't know. Well. There it is. It happened."

"Tell me everything. Slowly and in great detail," Bianca said, leaning forward eagerly, making Gwen chuckle. Soon they were gossiping about the merits of a good kisser like they were having a pint at the pub, not aboard a boat on a deadly mission. It was easy to forget, in these moments, that they were on a quest of the highest order.

"We should go up. I need to pull my weight – help with something," Gwen finally said, reluctantly ending the conversation.

"I know Seamus wants to hear about the mermaids as well. I've been dying to ask you, but certainly there was more fun information that needed to be discussed first," Bianca said, standing and stretching her arms above her head. "Listen, Gwen. Don't worry about what will happen with Loch. He's clearly a very stubborn man and set in his ways. Let things unfold as they unfold. You are an amazing person – all you have to do is be you. I suspect he's fallen further than you realize. But you can't force his hand. He needs to work through whatever it is that's holding him back from making a move on you. For now? I'd say sit back and enjoy the ride. See where this goes."

"I… I hadn't really had a plan with any of this. Last night was the first time I actually considered the fact that he might look at me as more than an annoying kid sister he has to protect. Though I've admired how handsome he is, I never really thought there could be more. Or hoped there would be. Now…" Gwen shrugged a shoulder. "I don't know if a kiss changes anything or not."

"It does," Bianca promised.

CHAPTER 26

*O*r not.

Gwen watched Loch as he stood at the helm, quietly discussing routes with Seamus, while she and Bianca leaned against the back wall of the narrow room and watched the waves slam into the hull.

He'd barely acknowledged her since they'd come in, simply giving her a cursory glance, his eyes stopping at the fleece coat, before turning back to Seamus. Men things, it seemed. Or fae things. Either way, it was getting a bit annoying that they weren't being included in the discussion.

"Should we maybe find some laundry to do or cook some meals?" Bianca asked sweetly, and Seamus turned with a broad grin on his face.

"Now, doll, you know that I love you and would never exclude you from anything. You're my heart, my soul, my light. We were just having a bit of chat, all of which I will of course fill you in on, if you would like."

Bianca dimpled at him. "I'd like."

Gwen almost sighed. The two were just so sweet together.

"My mate here was just telling me some of his tips and tricks for spells for breathing underwater. It's really quite fascinating, and I can see why it's taken him some time to even get to the point he has. He's lucky he lasted as long as he did last night – any longer and he'd be dead. But if he could master this? It could change the fae world as we know it and open up an entirely new realm for us to explore. Though we'd need to be having a bit of a chat or coming to an understanding with that family of yours," Seamus said, nodding at Gwen, who broke out in a smile.

"I'm sorry… it just still gives me thrills. Just to think of all of this – all this sitting right under my nose. Magick, and fae, and sirens, and mermaids… and, well, just wow. It's so fascinating to me and – well, exciting. It's just this amazing thing that has existed all along and I feel like a kid in a candy store. I want to know it all, taste it, live it, feel it – just absorb it, really." Gwen laughed at herself as she peered out at the stormy sea. Still no land on the horizon. She wondered how much longer they would have to travel.

"I second that," Bianca agreed. "I've been studying Celtic mythology and legends for years, and to find out that many of them are true and that they are alive and walking around right under my nose? It's like all my Christmases came at once."

"Hear that, Loch? We're nothing but a piece of candy or a present to be unwrapped to them. I hate how these women just objectify us all the time." Seamus let out a long exaggerated sigh, causing both women to laugh.

"Come here, cutie, and I'll objectify you all you want," Bianca said. Seamus willingly crossed the small room to receive a smacking kiss on the lips.

"Now, tell us every detail about the mermaids," Seamus

said, pulling Bianca back against him and resting his head on hers.

Gwen told them everything she could remember, savoring the imagery in her head, knowing that as long as she was blessed to live she would never forget that moment in the icy sea – surrounded by such beauty, with voices like nothing of this world singing a life-song just for her.

"Wait – they said they would fight for us below?" Loch interrupted her retelling of the story.

"She did say that. She said to have no fear of the water as they will fight for me. Or us, I suppose. I think they know of this quest we're on," Gwen said.

"I wonder how many beings are watching us," Bianca murmured, and Gwen tilted her head in question at her.

"You've got the whole world watching, more or less," Loch admitted.

Gwen whirled to look at him. "You can't mean that. Like we're some boxing match and people are betting on us?"

"People, leprechauns, mermaids – all the magickal beings are tuned in to this. I hope we'll continue to receive help along the way, as most everyone understands what a disaster it would spell if the Domnua were to once again run the world."

"Lep… leprechauns?" Bianca squealed and jumped up and down, almost knocking Seamus in the chin.

"Well, duh. Of course," Loch said, tossing her a smile before turning back to the window.

"I swear, this has been the best year of my life," Bianca squealed.

Gwen had to agree with her. They were on a real-life comic book quest and there was nothing that would tear her away from this moment.

"Well, if you feel that way, it's about to get more interesting. I believe we are on the right path to the Isle of Destiny," Loch murmured.

"Isn't that just another name for Ireland?" Bianca asked.

"It is. But not many know of the actual isle – it's magickal, and something quite tricky to find. That's what Seamus and I were discussing. We were trying to decide what might be the correct route to the isle. It's where the sirens supposedly once wrecked ships. It never shows up on radars or maps, and yet many claim to have seen it. But few leave it."

"Perhaps I could help?" Gwen asked timidly. "Maybe if I sing? Could I sing us there?"

"Aye, that's a thought. But would it also call down the Domnua again?" Loch asked, turning. Crossing his arms over his chest and leaning back, he studied Gwen. Happy to be included in the conversation, she didn't even let herself get annoyed at the fact that he was assuming her singing had brought the Domnua.

"We don't know that it was the song that brought them," Bianca protested.

"True. But is it worth the risk again?"

"Wouldn't it be best to do it on water? When we've got an army below, so to speak?" Gwen asked.

"Let's just think about this for a second," Bianca said. "Based on the clue that accompanied the bracelet – I suppose it could make sense. If this magickal island is a place of fire and ice, and there are sirens there or songs that caused people to follow along, it could make sense for Gwen to sing us in. And hopefully we get some guidance or ideas about where the spear is hiding."

"Um, but what if I sing and… you know." Gwen nodded her head at the men.

"I'll earmuff Seamus, don't you worry. Loch's your own problem," Bianca said cheerfully.

"Great," Loch and Gwen said at the same time.

CHAPTER 27

Gwen gripped the railing at the bow of the boat, feeling far less confident than she had when she'd first agreed to sing. Something that had once brought her joy, even quietly in the confines of her apartment, now was causing her great anxiety. Gulping, she stared out across the water to where the rollicking waves met the grey horizon, and wondered what she should sing.

Gwen glanced nervously over her shoulder to where Loch stood at the window of the bridge, his arms crossed, eyes trained on her. Seeming to sense her anxiety, he gave her a thumbs-up. Bianca had taken Seamus below deck with the promise to drown out her singing, so it was just the two of them on deck.

Swallowing, she gave Loch a little nod and then turned, once more facing the water. Yet still no song came. It was as though the fear of the last battle had rendered her unable to sing. The consequences seemed too great.

"Cat got your tongue?" Loch asked from behind her and Gwen stiffened, refusing to turn around. She was supposed to do her part on this journey, it would be an embarrassment if she froze now.

"I'll admit that I'm a bit worried about the consequences," Gwen finally said. She was surprised when Loch leaned against the railing, his shoulder bumping hers companionably. They stood that way in silence but for the waves slapping against the hull, the rocking of the boat seeming to soothe her fears a bit.

"My mother once told me the story of Carman, a Celtic witch. Have you heard tell of her?"

Gwen shook her head no, but was delighted that he was opening up more to her.

"Ah, well, she's quite the evil she-beast, that's the truth of it. One of those women who could never bear to see others happy, you know the type?"

Gwen nodded, relaxing as he wound into his story.

"And so, one day she was going about her path of destruction, particularly annoyed that the Goddess Danu had brought such joy and bountiful crops to the land. As Carman tooled along the land, the booming crops and cheerful people infuriated her. You see, for all the power she had, she was an unhappy woman deep inside." Loch brought his fist to his chest. "Unable to bear seeing the happy fae, the beautiful land, and a goddess bringing such joy to her people, she decided to bring her wrath to the lands. And so she did, in the form of a famine, one so great that it struck the land to its depths, sucking it dry and devouring all the great bounty that once was. Danu couldn't stop her, you see, because Carman was stronger than her."

"Oh no," Gwen said, caught in the rhythm of his voice as he wove the story for her.

"Oh no, indeed," Loch said. "So when the goddess

appeared to her people, the Danula themselves, and said she didn't know how to fight – the fae were dying, the food was gone, the earth's magick had waned to but a drop – do you know what they said?"

"They blamed her?"

"No, my dear, they did not. They stood up, one by one, and promised they would fight – for the life they had, for the future of their children's children, for the breath of magick that they still felt pulse deep within Mother Earth. And even knowing they might die or bring Carman's wrath down upon them tenfold, they rose up anyway, buoying Goddess Danu until she discovered what she should have already known."

"That she had been stronger than Carman all along?"

"Nay, she wasn't stronger all along. She was only more powerful once she believed she could win."

Gwen smiled, completely charmed by the story. There was something nice about Loch opening up about his mother, a warmth in his voice that she hadn't heard before.

"So what you're telling me is that great risks often come with great rewards."

"You can't tell me you expected this to be easy now, did you?" Loch said, laughing down at her.

Gwen found herself caught for a moment, her breath simply leaving her as she gazed up into his handsome laughing face. It was an image she would hold with her – this handsome fae sorcerer having dropped his guard for a moment, looking for all the world like a man with no burdens. He was holding her hand, helping her along, and not once did he make her feel ashamed of needing his help.

And so she sang, the first song that popped into her head, grateful it wasn't a love song, just on the off chance that if she sang of romance she might weave some spell she wouldn't know how to change.

"What would you think if I sang out of tune/Would you stand up and walk out on me? Lend me your ears and I'll sing you a song/and I'll try not to sing out of key," Gwen sang, softly at first, channeling the Joe Cocker version of the song, loving the music as it filled her body. "Oh, I get by with a little help from my friends…"

The words carried away from her, pulling through her body like magick, the song washing across the water as Gwen focused on her friends and being in the battle together. As the song filled the air, she sent up a prayer that the words she sang wouldn't be a death knell for her friends.

"You've done it, princess. Aye, would you just look at that," Loch shouted, and before Gwen could even take in the beauty of what lay before her, he'd claimed her mouth in a searing kiss, one that crossed all the circuits in her brain and stopped the song dead in its tracks.

With another whoop, Loch shouted to Bianca below deck and loped across the boat, once more taking his place at the helm. Gwen clapped a hand to her mouth, once again feeling his kiss linger on her lips, and found herself giggling before turning to look out across the bow.

To her destiny, which lay before her.

CHAPTER 28

"I've never seen such a thing in my life," Bianca breathed, standing next to her. Gwen refused to leave the bow, no matter the cold wind that whipped her curls madly around her head.

"It's like looking at an island through a snow globe or something," Gwen said, struggling for words to describe what she saw. "But it's snow and sun and warmth and cold... a blend of everything. And the air – it shimmers. See that? See how it shifts and shimmers?"

"Aye, that must be the magick we're seeing. Everyone else passing by would see naught but water," Bianca said, just as delighted with the vision as Gwen was.

It truly was a sight to behold. Gwen didn't know where to look first. It was as though she couldn't tear her eyes away but still couldn't take in enough details. On one end of the island, jagged cliffs, almost as black as night, presented a formidable barrier to those approaching from the east. Molten lava, orange as the setting sun, ran in rivulets down the black rock, collapsing into the sea with poofs of steam. Night hung like a shroud on this side of the island, complete with a slice of moon and a twinkle of stars in the dark sky. To the far west were hills of the greenest grass, hugging rounded cliffs of white rock, all protecting a golden sandy beach. The sun, though cheerful, was a bit hidden behind the clouds. It was still Ireland, after all. The overall effect was like looking at twenty-four hours of a day in one glance. It was yin to yang, black to white…

"Day by night," Gwen murmured.

"It is at that, isn't it. Black and white, light and dark, good and bad," Bianca murmured.

"Two sides to the same coin," Gwen said automatically, surprising herself. "The island mirrors the dichotomy that lies within all of us. We can go either way. Be our best self – take the high road – or listen to our bad sides. Nobody is bad or good all the time, but we do have choices. It's like a metaphor for humanity. I think the sirens have a curious sense of humor."

"That's… actually, that's an excellent way to see the island. Perhaps the only way that makes sense. Especially if it is named the Isle of Destiny. Because doesn't the very concept of destiny belie the fact that we can choose our destiny? Fate is believed to be inevitable, while destiny is something that a person can determine."

Gwen nodded in agreement.

"And so we choose – do we go the route of darkness or take the path of light?"

"I think the bigger question is, where would the spear be and, if it was hidden by fae in years past, what path would they expect us to take?"

"I'd say the light," Loch said from behind them, startling

them both. They turned to see Seamus and Loch listening avidly to their conversation.

"Brilliant observations, ladies," Seamus said with a smile as the boat crept closer to the island. "Brains and beauty – a winning combination that any man would be lucky to have on his arm."

Bianca twinkled at Seamus. "I'm proud to have you on my arm too, love."

"Why do you think the spear is on the light side of the island?"

"I think the fae would expect us to think they hid it on the scary side of the island, a place that looks more difficult to get to. But fae are tricky, so it's possible they put it on the light side instead." Loch shrugged.

"I think wherever it is, it will be in the place we least expect it to be, that's for sure. Each treasure so far has had an interesting way of surprising us. I think, for now, we should try and get as close as possible and assess the situation. Perhaps we'll find an easy entry point."

Seamus had a point. They quickly agreed to cruise in a circle around the island, giving the beaches and cliffs a wide berth until they had a better idea of the topography and what they were dealing with. None of them expected the island to be as large as it was, and it took almost two hours for them to circle the entire island, exclamations popping from their mouths every time they happened on a new discovery.

"How is it snowing on one side of the island, sunny on the other, green over here and molten lava over there?" Bianca threw up her hands in mock exasperation. "It's like an extra credit exam question they would give to a meteorologist. They'd never find an answer."

"Well, because the answer is magick," Loch said wryly, smiling down at the blonde.

Gwen caught herself staring at him again, mesmerized every time he smiled. It was like something had shifted in him and she couldn't quite resist stealing glances at him as he captained the boat.

A few times, he caught her eye and she found herself flushing, once again berating her porcelain skin before turning away. To her surprise, she found herself wondering about more than kissing him – about being cradled in his arms while he showed her the love of a man.

Love. Gwen rolled her eyes as the boat came around a rocky outcropping. That wasn't part of her and Loch's destiny, she was certain of that. But maybe, just maybe, she could have passion – something the man had in spades. Perhaps a night of passion on a magickal quest would be worth the battle they were fighting.

Because if she were to die one of these mornings, on a snowy expanse of magickal beach, then one night, oh yes, one glorious night she would have, to celebrate the bounty of life.

"here's shelter," Seamus cried, pointing to several stone cottages clustered on the hills in the center of the island. Whoever had built them had chosen the best spots for them, as they provided a good view, were in what appeared to be the consistently sunny part of the island, and were sheltered from the wind by a rocky outcropping.

"Was that there before? Haven't we circled the whole island?" Bianca asked. Gwen just shrugged. Time felt weird here, as if it were suspended or a bit slower.

"I thought we had, but now I don't know. I think we just need to be aware that we are in a land of high magick and that anything may be not what it seems," Seamus said.

Gwen nodded. "Like Alice in Wonderland."

"Without the magick mushrooms," Bianca snorted. Both men looked at them in confusion.

"Shut up," Gwen said, "Tell me you've read *Alice in Wonderland*."

"No clue." Loch shrugged and Seamus shook his head.

"I don't even know what to say to that," Bianca said.

"Except that when we get home, I have a book for you to read that is going to knock your socks off."

"Or a movie, if you go for that," Gwen said.

"Oh, films! I love films," Seamus said happily.

Gwen thought back to Loch's story about Danu's battle over Carman. It was nice to talk easily about films or books they would read when this was over. There had to be some magick in manifesting outcomes – in talking easily of the future after battle.

"How do you reckon we're to get to shore? Does this thing have a dinghy?" Seamus asked, and they all turned when they heard a splash. Loch had managed to procure a life raft from somewhere on the boat and had plopped it into the water next to the swim dock.

"I think we have a dinghy," Gwen said.

"Looks like that's indeed a dinghy," Bianca said solemnly.

They all snorted.

"What are you, five years old?" Gwen said, but laughed right along with them as they trooped below deck.

Loch had given the order that they bring only the necessary supplies, and since Gwen had little to nothing of her own as it was, she packed food that she thought would be best, and then carried it upstairs and to the swim dock. In no time, they were all standing at the swim dock and eying the dinghy. It looked considerably smaller now that it was stuffed full of boxes and supplies.

"I'm nervous to leave this boat. It's our only way out off of this island. What happens if this all disappears – and the boat along with it?" Gwen finally voiced the worry that had been niggling in the back of her head. Because prior to her singing, the boat had been cruising along in a thousand-plus feet of water, with nothing to secure it in place, and now it was anchored to the sea bottom of a magickal island that might or might not exist outside of her mind.

It was a bit daunting, to say the least.

"Didn't your mermaid family say they had your back? Wouldn't that include making sure our boat was kept safe?" Bianca pointed out.

Loch leveled a look at Gwen, causing her to nod once.

"Trust. Got it. Okay, then." Gwen blew out a breath and tucked a wayward strand of hair behind her ear. "Shall we explore the Isle of Destiny?"

"I thought you'd never ask." Bianca beamed at her and together they climbed into the dinghy, unhooking it from the yacht. Gwen whispered a soft plea to the sirens – or the goddess or anyone who would listen – to protect their safe passage in and out, before turning her eyes to the horizon. Onward they forged.

"Ahem. I hate to burst your bubble, ladies, but this is a life raft. Get to rowing," Loch said from behind them.

"You just can't get good help these days," Bianca complained, and they each hefted a paddle, turning the raft to shore.

Gwen found herself smiling the entire way in.

CHAPTER 30

*G*wen wasn't going to lie, she had a bit more than a moment of panic when they reached the beach and she turned around to see that the boat had disappeared.

"Shhh, it will be fine. It's there. I promise it's there," Loch soothed her, draping one arm casually over her shoulder and squeezing her to his side. His warmth eased her tension, but Gwen couldn't quite tamp down on the fear that raced through her.

"But how do you know?"

"It is. You have to have faith. Do you or do you not believe that the mermaids have your back?"

"I do… I guess. But what if harm came to them?"

"Then we are definitely screwed," Loch said and laughed at the devastation that crossed Gwen's face. "I'm kidding. It's fine. And we've got bigger things to worry about than the boat. It will be there when we need it. If not, fear for nothing. I have my ways."

Gwen had to remind herself that he was more than a normal man. "Right, you're a sorcerer. I keep forgetting."

Loch huffed out a breath in pretend irritation.

"This does not do much for my ego."

"I'm sorry. I'm still getting used to the people-wielding-magick-in-real-life thing," Gwen said, holding her bracelets aloft and smiling as they glinted in the sun.

"I wonder if they'll work the same here, or differently," Bianca said, coming to stand by them on the beach and looking at the bracelets.

"Like maybe the fire bracelet shoots fire because the ice bracelet shoots ice?" Gwen hoped so. That would be beyond cool.

"We'll let you test it out. Let's scope those cottages and see about securing shelter before we plan our next steps."

"Or you might be able to test them now," Seamus shouted. "Look out!"

Fear lanced through Gwen when she whirled to look at what Seamus was pointing at. It was as though a vertical crack had appeared on the horizon – the shimmer in the air parting to show what lay beyond. A parting of the veil, or curtains – Gwen's brain scrambled to keep up with what she was seeing – to show that, beyond this magick bubble they currently coexisted in, was pure chaos.

Thousands upon thousands of Domnua raged in the seas, clambering on boats and flying on winged serpents of death from the sky, shooting fiery bolts down from beasts of Armageddon.

"I don't understand – why are we just seeing a sliver of them?" Gwen shouted over to the others, who had raced to duck behind boulders. Realizing she was a sitting duck out on her own, she scurried after them.

"I think it's the magick of the island. They're trying to penetrate it, so we're seeing in real time what's happening outside this bubble. They know we're here, but they can't seem to get in."

"A few can," Seamus said, standing and easily picking off the Domnua that had managed to slip through the crack when it had briefly flickered open again.

"Do you think the magick will hold?" Gwen asked, clutching Loch's arm.

"It'll hold," Loch said, his eyes meeting hers. "But that's on you."

"I have to believe," Gwen whispered, wringing her hands.

"You have to believe. And use your magick. And sing a bit. And probably a whole slew of other stuff we don't quite know yet. But, aye, you should be using all the tools at your disposal. Don't think like a human anymore, remember?"

Loch's words held no censure, just a gentle prodding for Gwen to remind herself of the power she held within. She raised her arms, gasping when she saw the crack widen and glimpsed once more the turmoil that seethed outside their magickal realm.

"Just fix the snow globe," Gwen whispered to herself, and shot ice from her bracelets, freezing any Domnua that slipped through the gap and filling it until, once more, it was impenetrable.

"I have to admit, yours might be my favorite of the powers so far," Bianca said, breaking the silence that had fallen after Gwen's icy patch job. "It's crazy, because now you've created kind of a window out into the world beyond. Can you see? It's fuzzy, like looking through those glass blocks you see in showers sometimes, but you can kind of see the mess outside. But yeah, sealed right up," Bianca continued.

"Nicely done, princess," Loch said, winking at her before turning to climb the path that led to the cottages above them.

"I can't believe I just did that," Gwen said, shooting glances over her shoulder as they all traipsed up the hill, loaded down with their supplies. "I really... it's just kind of out of this world."

"In all fairness, we aren't really in the world right now anyway, are we?" Bianca said, cheerfully trudging up the slope. "We're in a parallel world. I'd say anything goes at this juncture."

To demonstrate her point, a lightning bolt struck close by and rain began to fall in a neat stream, while the sun shined happily mere inches away.

"See? Anything goes. Now, if the Cheshire cat pops out, I'd say we've gone and lost our damn minds."

"Fair enough. I'll keep an eye out for the cat. In the meantime, I need to revamp my way of thinking," Gwen said.

And consider the possibility that she might just be the most powerful one on the quest after all.

CHAPTER 31

*L*och watched Gwen, sensing a shift in her. Something almost imperceptible, but he found his eyes straying to her more often than he would have liked. The more she tested her power, the more confident she became.

A smile hovered lightly on her lips as she unpacked the supplies they'd brought into the cottage – which it seemed she and Loch were destined to share, since Seamus and Bianca had claimed the smaller one a ways down the hill. Though if Loch had any say in the matter, he was going to stay on watch tonight, invoking one of his favorite spells to give him energy so he'd be able to function without much sleep.

The alternative was to sleep with Gwen on the bed he'd glimpsed in the bedroom of the cottage – a massive four-poster bed with sweeping white netting strung between the posts, creating a lacy awning above the bed, which was piled with silky linens and pillows.

For an abandoned cottage in the middle of the hills, it certainly held some surprises. Loch wondered briefly whether it was a trap, or if it was simply Gwen's family's way of welcoming her home. He also wondered if she realized that it was their magic that kept them safe now, and that the sirens were likely still battling a war right outside the barriers of this island.

He glanced over at Gwen's delighted squeal.

"Look, Loch! Food rations, whiskey – oh, and even towels and soap for the bathroom!"

Oh yeah, her family had a hand in this. There was no way they'd let one of their own sleep on the floor. Which is exactly where he planned to sleep – on the floor on a bedroll, as far from the temptation Gwen presented as he could get.

He swore silently as he walked from the cottage, ostensibly to check the perimeter but more to try and clear his mind of Gwen. Her very essence seemed to seep into him every time he was near her. Even when he couldn't see her, he could feel her, taste her lips on his, see her naked body in his mind's eye. And what a cruel trick that had been this morning – walking in on her naked again.

It was as though the universe was having a laugh at him.

Her luscious curves begged to be touched – and by him. Loch gripped his hands tightly together as he thought about how her skin flushed when she got angry or embarrassed. He'd love to see her body glow, but from his touch, her lips swollen from his kisses, her skin pink from his attention.

Oh, she was the most cruel of temptresses, a woman who had yet to fully discover the power within, only waiting to be awakened to what she was.

And Loch knew he had the key. He had but to use it.

It wouldn't be fair to her to do so, he reminded himself, for the thousandth time, as he checked the locks on a window.

He was meant to be alone. No matter if his heart said she

was his mate, his mind knew better. He could be stronger than his heart, Loch promised himself.

He had to be.

CHAPTER 32

*A*s haphazard meals went, thrown together from what they had brought and what Gwen and Bianca had found foraging the hills around the cottages – staying within sight of the ever-watchful Loch – it was delightful. Crusts of bread with a honey drizzle, a fruit almost radiantly pink – unknown to any of them but delicious nonetheless – and heaps of nuts and seeds proved to be quite filling.

"Gwen, how do you know this fruit won't poison us?" Seamus asked again, and Gwen shrugged.

"I don't know for certain. But I just feel it."

"It's good. My gut response says the same," Loch said, taking a slice of the pink fruit and swallowing it down.

"That works for me then," Seamus said.

Gwen found herself smiling at everyone, content in these hills, watching the play of light and change of seasons swirl around them. It was as though she could sit back and watch a movie, except it was happening in front of her, in real time. If she craved the touch of snow, she had but to clamber over a few hills and cliffs and she would be among the ice. If molten lava interested her, which it did not, she needed only climb the other side of the mountain. But her eyes kept being drawn to a small beach, sheltered on all sides by steep cliffs, where moonlight created a single path of light – like a beacon – across the dark water.

She would go there, to this beach. This much she knew. But first, she'd wait for the others to rest. This was something she needed to do alone.

"Do you think we're safe tonight? As in, we can ease our watch and rest? Or is this the time when they'll pounce?" Bianca wondered aloud, taking a bite of honey-coated bread, her eyes closing briefly in ecstasy at the taste.

"I think we'd have fair warning of anything that comes our way," Gwen said. "Listen – can you hear their song?"

They all fell silent, and on the gusts of wind that rose from the shores below, through the moonlit waters and across the hills lit by sunshine, the mermaids' voices carried. It was a haunting song, one of war, yet one that spoke of honor and protection.

"It's beautiful. But why aren't we drawn to it? I mean, the men aren't racing down the hills to find these beautiful women. Would that mean they are mermaids, or sirens, or both? I'm not sure what to believe from myths, what is real, and, well…" Bianca gestured, indicating their surroundings, where three different seasons and times of day mixed and melded in their view. "Because this is all a little improbable."

"I think that, along the way, the myths and legends blend. And there is probably a kernel of truth to each. But the race found here? I'd say they are both sirens and mermaids. Their own particular blend, if you will," Loch said, leaning back against the grass to study Gwen. They'd set up the meal outside on the cliff in front of one of the cottages so they could continue to watch the beauty of the island dance in front of them, as well as keep an eye out for danger. It could've been a picnic on a lazy Sunday, except for the dramatic magick that wove its spell around their shoulders, as well as the knowledge that a war raged beyond the magickal barrier of the island.

"Perhaps it is the best of both? They get the powerful singing and the fun of being a mermaid, without having to slaughter men left and right," Bianca said.

Gwen laughed at her, delighted. She'd been feeling nothing but good vibes since she'd stepped on the island. It seemed to recognize its own and welcome her home.

"I think we should never underestimate them," Loch said softly.

"I agree," Gwen said. "It seems to me if they wanted to sing a song that would have you men panting at their feet in seconds, they could do so. It's a choice, an intention, and a judicious use of power. I'd say because of my blood and who I am, we are being protected. Probably because of who Loch is as well, though he himself said he wasn't sure of the relationship of the fae with the mermaids."

"Can we just call them that then? The mermaids? It sounds friendlier to me and less likely that I'll get eaten," Seamus said.

Gwen threw back her head and laughed. The sound seemed to echo down the sides of the cliffs, reverberating off the walls, and in moments they heard it reflected back to them, multiplied with the sound of those below, who laughed with her as they danced beneath the waves.

"Wow, just wow," Bianca breathed. "They like it when you are happy."

"Keep Gwen happy. Got it." Seamus nodded enthusiastically. "Anything we can do for you? A foot rub? More food? Whiskey? Does your bed need a turn-down, or can we carry you on our shoulders to the cliffs? We're at your command, O beautiful fairy of the sea," Seamus said, ducking his head and assuming the role of a hotel porter.

"Sea fairy – I like that." Gwen smiled at him.

"It's just as pretty as mermaid. And I can just see you, flitting through the water with that mass of curls around your head, shooting magic from your bracelets," Bianca mused, eyeing Gwen.

"Aye, I can see it too. Fairy of the sea, enchantress of all…" Loch murmured, his eyes locking with Gwen's. Her heart seemed to slow its beats for a moment, power zinging between the two of them until she felt heated to her core.

Bianca looked between the two as the silence drew out.

"I think that's our sign to be retiring to our cottage. Though it feels weird to try and sleep in the sunshine. I wonder if that's how people in Iceland feel during those long periods when the sun never really sets," Bianca babbled, nudging Seamus to get up when neither Gwen nor Loch looked their way.

"Right, right. Goodnight. We'll be sure to listen for any songs of warning or…" Seamus just trailed off as Bianca dragged him down the path, happy to be disappearing with his love to a remote cottage in the hills.

Gwen's eyes traced the stubborn set of Loch's jaw, his tawny eyes, now hooded as he looked down and then away. The man had so much honor, restraint, and a sadness inside him she'd yet to understand.

"I feel for you," Gwen finally admitted, feeling comfortable in this place of power, willing to be vulnerable to Loch.

She raised a fist to her core, right below her breasts. "Right here, I carry deep feelings for you. As though we are connected in a way that I can't explain or understand."

If anything, Loch's face only looked more mulish as he looked away over the sea.

"Is that not so with you? Am I the only one with these feelings?" Gwen asked softly, not moving, waiting to see if he would be honest with her and with himself.

"Ah, Gwen, you're a looker, that's the truth of it," Loch said, not meeting her eyes as he shrugged casually. "But I told you not to get ideas about me. Women always do. I'm not meant to partner with someone. It's best a sorcerer goes alone – so as not to get distracted. I hope you understand."

Gwen understood far more than he was saying, and she smiled in understanding. There was something about this place, and the power she felt here, that allowed her to see past his words to the truth that lay beneath.

Lochlain of the high royal fae had very deep feelings for her, but he was allowing fear – the fear of what could be – to stop him. It seemed the great sorcerer wasn't listening to his own lesson – that taking great risks yielded great rewards.

"Aye, I understand," Gwen said, and Loch sent her a relieved smile. "It's easy to get caught up in the passion of a quest and battles."

"That it is. I'm glad you're being reasonable about this."

"Of course I am. I would never want to give myself to someone who doesn't share the same feelings as I do," Gwen said, and rose while Loch all but choked on his whiskey at her talking so freely about her innocence. "I'm certain I won't have trouble finding those feelings again, now that I understand them so much better. Thank you for being patient with me and helping me to understand what is real and what isn't."

Gwen leaned down and brushed a sisterly kiss against Loch's cheek, almost laughing when she saw the man's fists clench in his lap. Unaffected? Not in the slightest.

"I'm going to get ready for sleep. You should rest as well. You're safe here."

CHAPTER 33

*G*wen bided her time, waiting until she was certain Loch was asleep before she answered the call that had been pulling her toward the moonlit beach far below the cliff their cottage stood upon. True to his word, Loch had insisted she sleep in the bed while he had found a spot in the grass outside, protected by boulders, with a beautiful arch of trees to shelter him from the sun, which still shone cheerfully behind little cotton-puff clouds drifting by.

She paused, smiling at Lochlain, and admired him for a moment in his relaxed state, his arms crossed behind his head, his tawny eyes hidden beneath closed lids. His broad chest rose in easy, even breaths, and Gwen ached to curl up next to him and put her head to his chest, to be held in those strong arms.

Later, she promised herself.

Gwen padded silently past him, her feet bare, and made her way quickly down the path that hugged the side of the cliffs. She slipped seamlessly from sunshine to moonlight, turning once to admire the gradient of day to night behind her. The wind slowed as she neared the moonlit shore, and silence greeted her, but for the gentle lap of waves. Gwen smiled, reaching her arms up toward the moon, delighting in the way the light scattered across the surface of the water, a thousand crystals thrown across a ribbon of blue velvet.

Gwen dug her toes into the sand, allowing the water to caress her feet, aching to swim in the water. But she wouldn't, not now, for her heart also lay with those who slumbered in the cottages far above. It wouldn't be fair to them to risk swimming when she was still uncertain of who and what she was. Though every moment of this quest brought her closer to understanding her own personal power, she had others to think of. To risk herself in the sea would only put them in peril if they needed to save her.

Gwen contented herself with enjoying the feel of the water at her feet, the light of the moon caressing her face, and the dull beat of the magick of the island pulsing in her core. Its blood called to her blood, and she knew one day she would come back to this place.

She turned, a smile on her lips, to greet the woman who rose from the water. Naked, her porcelain skin a mirror of Gwen's own and her thick curls winding around her shoulders to her waist, the woman raised her arms to the sky and cloaked herself in a gown of gossamer moonlight, the folds shifting and shimmering around her curves, as she glided toward where Gwen stood.

Instinctively, Gwen bowed her head when the woman stopped in front of her.

"I am Amynta, defender of the Isle of Destiny, and mother to your blood," the woman said, a soft smile playing across her luminous face.

"Mother to my blood," Gwen breathed, raising her head

to meet Amynta's eyes, a mirror of her own. "It is an honor to meet you."

Amynta inclined her head regally, a warrior acknowledging her young.

Knowing that to hug this woman would be an insult to what she was, Gwen contented herself with memorizing every detail of her mother, feeling strength fill her as she finally understood the magick from which she was formed.

"You've fared well, I see, in this human form. Come, walk with me," Amynta said. They both turned to stroll the beach, and in another life they would have been simply a mother and daughter, walking by the water on a beautiful evening.

"I have. Though it has been a delight to discover that there is more to me than I knew," Gwen admitted.

"Your gran? She cared for you well?" Amynta asked.

"She's wonderful. I couldn't have had a happier upbringing," Gwen gushed.

"That eases me. I've often thought of you and wondered if you had happiness. It is a feeling we prize, among our people. Though we understand and deal readily in the darker side of life, happiness and joy are to be treasured."

"I've known happiness. I've wanted for nothing," Gwen said. She smiled at Amynta and was rewarded with a kind smile back.

"Then I made the right choice, to give you up."

"Why did you, then?" Gwen gulped, feeling surprised at her audacity, but she figured it was now or never to get answers. Not that she needed them, but it would certainly add another chapter to her own personal story.

"It's a fair question, and one that I will answer," Amynta said, inclining her head once to Gwen. "Our people, you understand, have difficulty conceiving. Typically, only royalty can carry on the bloodline, but that still gets diluted. Once in a while, we'll have mermaids with great fertility, and the royals allow them to birth their children as they still want diversity in our bloodline."

About a gazillion questions popped into Gwen's head, but she instinctively knew that this was a time to just listen.

"While we choose lovers freely, as we believe in celebrating joy, there are some sacred rules."

"There are men then?" Gwen blurted out. She kept picturing the mermaids and sirens as a great community of Amazonian-type women ruling the sea.

"Of course there are men. We women are equal to if not stronger than them, however." Amynta laughed softly. "It is a society that very much celebrates the feminine divine power, and we are given full rein to use our gifts as we see fit."

"I see. I like that," Gwen said, kicking her foot in the water a bit.

"It is a society that is not without its troubles. We celebrate joy, but we understand pain, anger, and jealousy just as well. And jealousy is what drove my decision to give you a safe home."

"You were jealous of someone?" Gwen asked.

Amynta tossed her head back and laughed, the beautiful sound like a thousand stars twinkling in the sky, and shook her head in dissent.

"No, my beauty, I was not jealous of someone. But someone was of me."

"Ah," Gwen said.

"You see, there are many royal houses in our society, and with them come many a princess."

"Are you a princess?"

"I'm not. I'm something outside the royal family – an untouchable, if you will." Amynta seemed to search her mind for the right wording. "As a defender of our people, I'm... would you say a goddess? I'm not necessarily required to follow the ruling of the royal people, but often do so in order to keep the peace. However, should I need to make a decision that benefits the society as a whole, even if it usurps a decision made by one with royal blood, I may do so without consequence."

"You're a peacekeeper."

"Yes, while often having to use violence to do so. It is not always an easy life, sustaining these magickal beings and defending an isle not known to many. Our way of life is dying, and it is only through great care and perseverance that we can continue our society."

"I'm still amazed to learn that there are so many magickal beings existing outside of what humans know," Gwen admitted. "I've always been drawn to stories about them – but to find out they are real? And I'm one of them? It's astounding. I can't even imagine how difficult it is to keep this island free from discovery."

Amynta inclined her head, gracefully accepting the compliment, and continued with her story.

"We don't always do well with it. We're a curious bunch, which is why there are myths and legends that exist about mermaids. We wander afar. I wandered one day. Which is when I met your father."

"A fae."

"Yes, a fae. A royal fae, at that. He'd been exploring the coast on a small boat, and I couldn't resist him, you see." Amynta half-laughed, a dreamy smile on her face. "He was so handsome – striking blonde hair and ice-blue eyes. I allowed him to see me, flitting below the surface. Instead of showing fear, he smiled, and beckoned me closer. Feeling no fear, I swam to him and held onto the side of his boat. We spoke for hours that day, and many days after. I began to look for him, straying farther and farther from my post to find him. You see, love will do that to you. It is a power above all others, causing you to put that love before anything else. One day he led me to a small island off the coast, a magickal one not known to humans, and we were together. Our love created you." Amynta smiled at Gwen.

"What… what happened next? Did you see him again?"

"I did. And we were both ecstatic about the pregnancy. In both our cultures, a child is to be considered a blessing – a gift of great joy. We discussed how your birth could be a bridge between our people, perhaps opening up a new way of life and a new treaty of peace and understanding. Though we'd lived side-by-side for years, the fae and the merpeople kept separate. Wisely so, I suspect," Amynta said.

"But someone was jealous of you."

"A royal princess, one who could not get pregnant. She came to me, the court at her side, insisting she would take you as her own and forbidding me from seeing your father again. Now, as I told you, I have the power to ignore the royals' demands. But you must understand the weight of fear and how it can wreak havoc in a society." Amynta shook her head and looked out to the moonlit water. "And those of the old way still feared the fae. Either I could give you to the princess or they would kill you in fear that you would bring bad magick to the island."

"But how would the princess have changed that if she had raised me? Wouldn't I still be of fae blood?" Gwen asked.

"I said they were powerful. I didn't say they were rational."

Gwen thought of the nature of the world's political climate, and could only agree with that statement.

"When it was time for your birth, my sister and I snuck away, and she helped me to the island where your father and I first met. I gave birth to you beneath the stars and handed you off to him. You see, he'd promised me he would ensure your safety, and I trusted him to do so. And he did, as I am speaking with you now," Amynta said, a faint smile still playing on her lips as she spoke of her great love.

"But why didn't the fae keep me?"

"It wasn't meant to be. The Goddess Danu knew you had a higher purpose, as a Seeker, and as such she hid you away for your safety until the time was right. But you must know, my child, starshine of my heart –" Amynta turned and placed her hands on Gwen's shoulders, her touch sending shivers of magick through Gwen's body – "you were born of love and you are loved. Every decision that was made was out of love. Remember that, as you travel this quest. It will serve you well."

"Did you... do you... still speak to my father? What of your love?"

Amynta shook her head and dropped her hands, bringing one palm to her chest.

"Love, once given, lives on. He lives in here, though we can no longer be together. I am content, my child. I've known great love, which is more than many can say. And what of you? Where is your great love? I feel it – inside of you. Where is this man?"

"He, like my father, is fae," Gwen admitted. "And he sleeps up on the cliffs as we speak."

"Why have you not been with him? Time is precious and tomorrow is promised to none. You must take love where it is given."

"He won't give it. He refuses to believe it and I don't know why," Gwen admitted, digging her toe into the sand, ashamed at being rejected.

"Ah, you've yet to give him your love. You must do so, freely," Amynta said, gently chiding Gwen.

"I told him that I have feelings for him," Gwen protested.

Amynta threw back her head and laughed once more, the waves dancing around her in joy as she did.

"Feelings are many. Love is everything. Go, tell him. Better yet, show him. Your love is a worthy gift and, when given freely, one that will forever change a man. Trust it."

Gwen closed her eyes for a moment, letting the truth flow through her. She did love Lochlain of the Fae, though she had known him but a short time. What was time when her heart recognized its mate in another?

"Be well, my child. It does my heart good to know you are safe. Remember who you are, the blood that flows through you," Amynta said, turning to brush her lips across Gwen's brow before slowly backing into the water. "You've but to call for me, and I will come. My love lies within you."

Gwen smiled, a piece of her heart feeling full in a way she had never had, and she raised one hand in goodbye as Amynta dove into the sea, a shimmer of colors beneath the surface, before the sea was once again empty.

Gwen turned her eyes to the cliffs and smiled.

CHAPTER 34

*L*och was awake when she returned, pacing in front of the cottage, the look on his face mutinous.

"How nice of you to return, princess," Loch said, his voice heavy with sarcasm. Gwen smiled at him, amused, and patted his cheek as she breezed past into the cottage and straight back to the bedroom, confident that he would follow to have his say.

"You may think you can do whatever you want, but you actually can't. There are other people to consider, people whose lives you can put in danger if you just wander off like you don't have a care in the world. What would have happened if you had been attacked by the Domnua? The quest would be over," Loch seethed from behind her.

Gwen turned, the smile still on her face. "But I wasn't. And you followed me anyway, so I knew I was safe."

"How did you know I followed you?" Loch asked, a dangerous glint in his eyes.

"Because I feel you, Lochlain of the Fae," Gwen said, bringing her hand to her heart, and stepping closer until she was only inches from him. "You and I – we are connected. Don't you feel it too?"

Gwen reached out and placed her hand on his chest, caught for a moment by the way the muscles rippled under her hands, feeling the beat of his heart under her palm. Slowly, she tilted her head until her eyes met his.

"Gwen," Loch said, and it was both an answer and a plea.

"I love you, Lochlain. Beyond all doubts, I love you. I give to you my heart, to do with as you will," Gwen said, humbling herself to him. At the same time, she discovered what power lay within being vulnerable – in opening her heart – and the beauty that was found in the tenuous threads of hope existing in that space. As the moment drew out, Gwen kept her eyes on Loch and waited.

"This isn't a good idea. Love is but a distraction from the quest. We need to stay focused," Loch said, but his protests sounded weak even to himself.

"Don't you think love will make us stronger? It's easier to fight the dark with the light," Gwen said, and tentatively, ever so slowly, she stood on her tip-toes and brushed a kiss across his lips. Softly, at first, but when he made no move to stop her, she pressed her lips harder to his.

The moment hung between them, the pain of her unanswered question drawing out until Gwen almost stepped back, but then he dove his hands into her hair, pulling it from its pins so that it toppled down her back.

"Ah, Gwenith, fairy of the sea, enchantress of my heart, I love you as well. I have been drawn to you since the moment that I saw you. Your resilient spirit, ability to laugh in the face of darkness, and lush beauty captivate me. I didn't want this – and I can't promise you forever. But I can give you my love, in this night, in this moment – I will honor you and our feelings."

It was enough for Gwen, for ultimately, who can promise tomorrow? She didn't need or want the promise of forever when they might very well die in the morning. Warmth filled her, and a new power, one unknown to her, made her step back. Eyes on his, she pulled her shirt over her head and quickly removed her pants. Standing there, naked as he'd seen her twice before, she flushed, uncertainty filling her for the first time since she'd kissed him.

"Gwen, you stop my heart. I've ached to touch you since I met you. You've no clue the beauty or power you hold," Loch said, stepping forward and wrapping his arms around her, claiming her mouth once again with his own. "I wondered why you dressed like you hated your body, but now I'm grateful you did. For you have kept the most beautiful secret private, for me to explore."

Gwen shivered at his words, but she had no fear. Loch was nothing if not honorable and she trusted him to show her how to love.

She gasped as he trailed a hand down to cup one of her breasts, palming it gently, as new sensations coursed through her, a liquid heat that made her squirm. Gently, he prodded her lips open with his tongue, tasting and teasing, never breaking his rhythm, as he slowly walked her back toward the bed, easing her down on the silken sheets.

"I want to touch you," Gwen said, pulling back from his kiss to meet his eyes, which had turned molten. She tugged gently at his shirt, needing to touch his skin, to see him. Understanding, Loch stood and quickly divested himself of clothing, standing before her all rippling muscle and proud maleness. Gwen swallowed as her eyes trailed down his body, and she gulped. There was no way they would fit together.

Unable to help herself, she traced her hands over the hard muscles of his chest, down over the ridges of his abs, and, looking up at him with a question in her eyes, even lower when he nodded. Delighted, she explored with such enthusiasm that he finally cuffed her hands and brought them to his lips, kissing them before pinning them over her head. Easing himself down until his weight pressed her to the bed, Loch began his own exploration.

Gwen shuddered as his lips found a sensitive spot at her neck, and he nuzzled in, blowing a warm breath against her skin before nibbling lightly at her ear. Capturing her lips in a searing kiss once more, Loch stayed there until Gwen began to moan against his mouth, her hips beginning to move of their own accord, aching for something she didn't yet know.

"Soon, my love, soon," Loch promised, and trailed kisses down her neck until his lips discovered her breasts. It was as though it was the first time he'd seen such a sight, and Gwen's eyes almost rolled back in her head. He spent considerable time and attention there, until she was shaking beneath him, wanting him so much she could barely breathe, and they'd only just begun.

"Please... I need..." Gwen found herself begging, her hands tangled in his hair, her hips arching from the bed.

"I will show you what you need, my beautiful Gwen," Loch whispered as his lips trailed over her stomach, finding the soft flesh of her thighs, then parting her where she most wanted him. Unable to hold back, the new sensation of being loved like this took her over the edge and, riding a wave of pleasure that was so strong her back bowed from the bed, she sobbed her release.

"You've enchanted me, my mistress of the seas," Loch gasped, kissing his way up her body and taking her mouth once more in a kiss made deeply intimate by the way he pressed himself against her. "I will forever cherish this gift you've give me – this moment we have."

Gwen sobbed against his mouth as he took her innocence, but in return gave her his heart. For there was nothing truly lost, when love was gained.

CHAPTER 35

*L*och smiled while Gwen enjoyed another first later that evening – bathing with a man. Delighted to find a huge tub in the attached bathroom, she sighed as Loch washed her body, lazily soaping her and paying careful attention to where she was most tender.

"Is it always this way? Does it always feel so good?" Gwen asked, tilting her head to look at him with love.

"No, it's not always this way. Sex is, of course, pleasurable. But there is pleasure for the sake of quick release and then there is a deeper pleasure – love, both physical and emotional – that makes it what battles are fought for and legends made of."

Gwen gazed at the man across from her, hopelessly besotted, and smiled at him. Loch saw the look, one of true love, and felt the nervousness slip through him once more. He wasn't sure whether he was scared because he'd seen his mother mourn the death of his father for years and had vowed never to love like that, or if it was because of what he had been told, by a great seer, was his destiny.

Either way, he loved this woman before him – yet he should have had better restraint, for he could never be with her. Not truly. And it wasn't fair to her, Loch thought, as she chattered away, glowing with love and happiness, all flushed skin and lush curves, her earlier nervousness about being naked around him now gone.

"Tell me about your family," Gwen said, eerily zeroing in on what he'd been thinking of.

"It's just my mother and myself," Loch said, picking up the sponge again to wash lazy circles around her breast, causing her breath to hitch a bit.

"Hatched from an egg, were you?" Gwen asked.

Loch smiled at her, though sadness washed through him when he thought of his father. "No, my father passed on. Killed in a great battle, years past."

"I'm sorry," Gwen said, reaching up a hand to touch his face, her look of concern genuine.

Loch felt that pull wash over him – wanting to lay his head down on her breast and let her hold him – before dismissing it. He was supposed to be the Protector, not her. He didn't need her comfort.

"It was harder watching my mother mourn, I think," he said.

"I can imagine. Was it a great love between them?"

"One for the ages," Loch said, and continued to wash her, keeping his eyes on her body and not her face.

"That's a terrible loss to have lived through, then. Especially as a child, to try and fill that gap of loneliness. I'm sorry for that," Gwen said, once again seeing unerringly through him.

"Aye. It's why loving to that level isn't smart," Loch said, knowing his words would be harsh after what they'd just shared, but needing her to understand where his hurts came from. "It's foolish."

Gwen opened her mouth to say something, but Loch cut her off, slanting his mouth across hers and trailing his hands over her body, driving her ruthlessly to the peak so that she gasped and shuddered beneath him. Then, picking her up from the tub, he carried her to the bed and loved her with an intensity that she would remember forever.

For in the morning, he would have to walk away before he shattered her innocent heart, which even now dreamed of a future together.

CHAPTER 36

"Good morning, handsome," Gwen said, rolling over in bed and delighted to see Loch moving around the room, packing their gear. "Perhaps you'd like to come back to bed?"

"No time for that. It's best to keep moving. Even if your family is holding the Domnua at bay, it isn't fair of us to leisurely while the day away when they are out there dying for our cause."

Stung, Gwen pulled the sheet around her and stood, making her way to the bathroom. She stopped at the door and turned to look at him.

"I'm well aware we are mid-battle, but my mother herself said to seize moments – moments that matter – and last night mattered. At least to me."

Loch sighed and scrubbed his face, looking mutinous.

A warning sounded in her head. "Or am I foolish to think it was meaningful?"

"Listen, I know a lot of things were said in the heat of

passion…" Loch began, and Gwen held up a hand, the other one gripping the sheet tightly around her.

"Don't. Don't do this. Not to me," she said, her chin held high and her eyes burning with unshed tears.

"Last night was great, sure, but as I told you – this isn't forever. I had a nice time and I know you did as well. I thought it was important that your first time be with someone who took the time to care for you and show you what love can be like."

"There's that pesky 'love' word again," Gwen said, her voice hitching. She would not cry.

Loch ran his hand through his hair, looking decidedly uncomfortable, and kept glancing toward the door.

"Gwen, I think you are incredible. But I can't be with you. Do you understand that? It's best all round if we leave it at what it was. A beautiful night we can look back fondly on years from now. It's time to get back to this battle, find the spear, and finish this up. Our people need us."

Gwen stared at him, a million things racing through her head. She wanted to scream at him that he was lying, she knew it – he'd felt something. Nobody could love another the way he had and remain untouched at his very core. She just didn't understand why he was doing this. Gwen thought to Amynta, how proud she'd been, and how easily she'd explained that love, once given, would always live in her heart. She'd given Loch her love last night, and no matter what might come, it lived in him. As his lived in her.

"You're right, Loch. Our people do need us. Thank you for the reminder, and I'll be certain to not distract you from the quest from now on. Perhaps you should go check the perimeter while I finish packing our supplies?"

A look of relief passed over Loch's face, which stabbed

Gwen to her core. Relief that she wasn't going to make a big drama about this, relief that he could move on without her. Despite trying to channel Amynta, pain coursed through her.

"I would suggest, though..." Gwen said, making Loch stop at the door and turn, "that the next time a woman bares her heart to you, you're more careful in your response. It's not kind, and I did expect more kindness from you. But, at least now I know what to avoid in my next lover."

The dark storm that flashed violently over Loch's face at the mention of her taking another lover only solidified what she felt inside. The man loved her and he was being an idiot. But why?

Frustrated, she let the tears come in the shower, and made a promise to herself that she would try to keep her heart open – no matter what lay ahead – as Amynta had reminded her she would need to do on this journey.

And so she would fight, for the spear and for love, and for all those who dared to believe in happy ever afters.

CHAPTER 37

*S*houting drew Gwen from the cottage at a dead run, her head whirling in every direction until she spotted Seamus and Loch in a standoff at the edge of the cliffs. When Seamus drew back a hand to punch Loch, Gwen almost screeched, but was scared to distract them lest they fall.

They were too far away for her to hear what they said, but Gwen had an idea of what it was about. Loch dodged the blow and turned his back on Seamus, and Gwen watched in disbelief as he slung a pack over his shoulder and took off across the ridge of the mountains and disappeared from sight.

"What the hell?" Gwen breathed.

"Oh, Gwen, are you okay?" Bianca bounded around the side of the hut and threw her arms around Gwen, pulling back and clucking like a mother hen as she studied Gwen's face.

"I'm fine, I'm fine. What's going on? Why the fighting?" Gwen asked, peering over Bianca's shoulder to see Seamus stalking back to them, his usually sunny face cloaked in rage.

"Loch told us about last night – and about how he'd left

things with you. He told us to watch out for you and that he couldn't be near you anymore. Seamus had a fit. Landed a few good punches, too – not that Loch put up a fight."

"He what?" Gwen choked. He'd taken their private moments and told others about them?

"When Seamus pressed him on why he was leaving, he told us. I'm so sorry, honey. Are you okay? What can I do for you? Did he at least treat you well? I guess that's a stupid question based on this morning, but you know what I mean – was he gentle? Oh, I can't believe I'm asking this stuff. I'm just so worried for you right now," Bianca said. She patted Gwen's arms helplessly, looking so miserable for her that Gwen sighed and pulled her into a hug.

"I'm fine. I really am. He showed me an amazing night and I will deal with the pain of this morning. After all, I come from a long line of warrior goddesses and all that, right? Heartbreak may be new to me, but it certainly isn't something that I can't handle," Gwen said, and felt grateful for Bianca when she gave an extra tight squeeze before stepping back. They both turned to look at Seamus, who stood looking about as awkward as a man could, all but wringing his hands as he tried to figure out what to say.

"Seamus. Thank you for defending my honor. It wasn't necessary, but I appreciate it," Gwen said, trying to put him at ease. "I'm strong enough to handle this."

Seamus studied her for a moment and, seeming to see what he needed to see, he nodded.

"It's right shite, that's the truth of it. No way to be treating a lady such as yourself," Seamus said, shaking his head as he pulled their supplies onto his back. Silently, they each took a pack and then turned to look around them.

"I suppose we should head in the direction he went? Or

go the other way?" Bianca said, nodding angrily toward where Loch had disappeared into the hills.

"Fire and ice," Gwen murmured, pointing to where molten lava met snowcapped peaks. "We might as well start with fire."

They trudged along in silence for a while, partly because the view was so astounding it was difficult to take it in, and partly, Gwen thought, because they felt awkward about what had transpired between her and Loch. Her tender muscles reminded her of their night with each step they took, and she did her best to cast her mind to any other topic. As they seamlessly left the sunshine behind and stepped into the moonlit part of the island, Gwen pointed down to the beach below them.

"I met my mother last night," she said.

Bianca gasped, turning toward her with delight. "Tell me everything."

By the time Gwen had wrapped up the story, Bianca's eyes were practically bugging out in delight at the new information about the mermaids, while Seamus had what seemed to be a look of dawning understanding on his face.

"I remember now… about Loch's father. This is beginning to make sense," Seamus said and Gwen's stomach dropped.

"I swear to god, if you tell me that Loch's father is my father too, I will push you off the side of this mountain," Gwen bit out.

"What? No! God, no. Sorry if I gave that impression," Seamus said, a smile flitting across his face for the first time since she'd seen him yesterday.

"What about his father? He told me that he died."

"He did. It is one of the most widely known stories of our

people, actually. I've told you that Loch is a great sorcerer, no?" Seamus said, and they settled in to listen to the story, slowly making progress along the ridgeline, the full moon lighting their way.

"Well, his family is known throughout the Danula. Most notably his father is legendary for the advances he made for our society and the great magicks he wielded in the face of major threats to the fae. I'm talking top-level stuff, the type of things you hear of in legends and myths."

"His father was big magick then," Bianca said.

"Aye, he was. And his mother – oh, she is one of the great beauties of the fae, one of the most sought-after women in our history. But she had eyes only for Loch's father. They had one of those love matches that transcends time. Unfortunately, his mother was tricked one day, by some very dark magick."

The skin prickled at the back of Gwen's neck. "Tricked how?"

"You see, they'd been trying for more children – as you know, it is tough for fae to conceive and carry children. Loch was still young, maybe seven or so, and his mother desperately wanted more children. She'd gone to a healer she'd heard tell of, far from our realm, and the healer promised strong magick to help her fertility."

"Oh no," Bianca whispered.

"His mother readily agreed, not knowing that the oath she signed was one of blood magick. As in, she would trade her own life to bear another child. You see, the dark magick was wielded by Nasslirus – those who collect the souls of great beauties and powerful wizards to form a parallel realm of their own making."

"His father tried to kill the Nasslirus?"

"Well, yes. In a way. See, they did conceive, and one day, as they were nearing the time of birth, happy as can be, a black bird – black as night – came to their door and delivered the message of doom. That the day of birth would also be a time of death."

"Oh... oh no." Gwen shook her head.

"And his father intervened. He traveled to the realm and found the witch doctor, sacrificing himself on the spot, before Loch's mother could protest, before anything could be changed. He knew how blood magick worked. The problem was, the contract was airtight. The Nasslirus was delighted – now he would get a much more powerful soul than Loch's mother. His mother has mourned the loss heavily her whole life. No matter what suitors came to her, no matter what magicks were offered to soothe her soul, she's never taken them. Instead she's committed herself to helping others and looking after Loch and his sister with a fierceness one might almost deem insufferable if there wasn't such tragedy behind it."

Gwen felt sick to her stomach. Her heart ached for this woman she didn't even know and the poor young boy who had lost his father.

"Now, it seems, he would do anything for her. His father made the ultimate sacrifice in the name of love, and Loch would do the same, I suppose. Which, by my guess, is why he is refusing to love you," Seamus said, his mouth twisted in sadness.

"But he does love me," Gwen insisted. "I can feel it. I know he does."

"Then why is he running from you? For a man who takes honor so seriously..." Bianca trailed off and shook her head.

"He's here as a punishment. He broke a sacred law,"

Gwen blurted out. She had kept his secret, but it seemed all bets were off when it came to secrets anyway. "Do you know what that could mean?"

Seamus stopped so suddenly that they all bumped into him, a domino effect that almost toppled them off the side of the mountain.

"I have heard tell of a sacred law being recently broken. There were whispers that the Goddess Danu's blood was taken. But for what, and by whom, nobody knew. We all assumed the perpetrator was put to death as immediate punishment," Seamus said, shaking his head in confusion. "But for what reason would Loch do that?"

"What does the blood do?" Bianca asked curiously.

"It's said to instantly heal those who are on their deathbed."

Bianca and Gwen turned to look at each other.

"He saved his mother," Bianca said.

Gwen gazed off across the hills, where moonlight filtered over molten lava running in rivulets down the side of craggy cliffs. Realization slammed into her so suddenly it made her gasp for air. Reaching out, she clenched Bianca's arm.

"He's going for the spear on his own. He's trying to save me from harm. Just like his father did for his mother."

"That idiot," Bianca shouted, then sighed, "But also, how romantic."

"'How romantic'? He'll get himself killed. He has no idea the powers of this island!" Gwen almost screamed in frustration. "Damn the man for having to do everything on his own. Doesn't he realize we are in this together?"

"I don't know if he has ever really had someone to be 'together' with, you know?" Seamus asked. "Aside from his mother who tried to give him everything, he's taken care of any real challenges on his own. Including taking care of his mother and saving her life. He makes the decisions. He's not accustomed to having a family to look out for him. Being on a team."

"Well, he's about to get a rude awakening," Gwen said fiercely, looking out to the lava once more. "Watch out, Lochlain of the Fae. You've got some serious lessons to learn about being a team player."

CHAPTER 38

"*H*ow can you know where he went?" Bianca grumbled, sweat running down her face as they carefully made their way over jagged black rock, dodging the rivulets of lava.

Gwen turned and grinned – an almost maniacal grin, she was sure of it – and tapped her chest. "I feel it. In here."

"Whatever you say, Sea Fairy, but can you channel him and tell him to keep away from the lava, maybe? This stuff is ridiculously hot," Bianca complained.

Seamus snorted. "Maybe that's why they always refer to it as molten lava?"

"You're lucky you're cute," Bianca grumbled, but blew Seamus a kiss anyway.

Gwen smiled, but her focus had gone inward. An energy seemed to hum through her, one of truth and rightness, and she tuned into it, knowing that deep down, love conquered all. Keeping her heart open, she let it draw her step by step, closer to where she knew Loch to be.

Bianca continued to complain, but good-naturedly.

"You'd think I would lose some weight with all this hiking and battling I've been doing." It was a tough hike, and had Gwen not been hiking the hills her whole life, she was certain she'd be in rough shape. Bianca's chatter didn't require a response, but it was easy background noise, so she half-listened as they made their way up each steep ascent, only to find another after it. And so it went, until even Seamus was red in the face and puffing from exertion.

"Air's thin up here," he said.

Gwen nodded, barely able to speak, so focused was she on finding Loch and trying to breathe. She knew he was close. "We have to keep going," Gwen urged, feeling panic creep up her spine. Whirling, she looked behind them. Below them the waves crashed in the moonlight, swallowing the red streams of lava, looking for all the world like the mountain was bleeding into the ocean.

"Something's wrong. Let's move," Gwen insisted, and began to run, rocks scattering beneath her feet and tumbling hundreds of feet into the water far below them.

"Gwen! Slow down! You'll fall!" Bianca screeched, but Gwen kept moving, as sure-footed as she'd ever been. She instinctively knew these mountains, as they were born of her people's blood. Leaping over the top ledge, she skidded to a halt, her hands coming automatically to her face in horror.

The Domnua had split the magickal barriers, and poured forth onto the tip of the mountain as though a dam had burst wide open.

And Loch stood, his arms raised to the sky, battling them on his own.

"You've got to be kidding me," Bianca screeched from behind her. "Of all the hot-headed stupid male things to do, to storm off on your own and battle this? How is he helping anyone by getting his ass killed? And for what? Stupid honor, stupid men! I swear to god I'm going to kick his ass myself when this is over," she said, and, raising her dagger, charged past an astounded Gwen and dove right into battle.

"She's something, isn't she?" Seamus grinned, bow and arrow at the ready, and began to pick off the Domnua that got through Loch's spell and came too close to his love.

Despite everything, Gwen found herself laughing as she plunged headlong into the battle of her life – for love.

CHAPTER 39

"Get out of here," Loch bit out, furious when Gwen plunged into battle next to him, bracelets raised as she began trying to ice the crack in the barrier closed. Realizing it was futile to try and close the ever-widening gap, she instead turned her attention to picking off the Domnua that ranged closer to the peak they stood upon.

"Like hell I will. We're in this together, you and I," Gwen argued as she admired Loch's use of spells to mow down wave after wave of Domnua.

"It's my job to protect you," Loch argued back.

"And it's my job to find the spear – not yours. I love you, Lochlain. You don't get to battle this alone. That's what love means, tackling the hard stuff together." Gwen ducked as an arrow breezed past her head. "And I'm quite certain this qualifies as the hard stuff."

"You're crazy, you know that?" Loch said, annoyance flitting across his face as he threw another spell across the peak, this one rumbling the mountain below them so that the

Domnua tumbled off the side and crashed to their deaths on the jagged rocks far below.

"Crazy about you," Gwen said cheerfully, throwing a bolt of ice at a Domnua that was too close to Bianca, who waved a cheerful thanks in response.

"I can't live if you get hurt," Loch finally yelled. "I can't lose you, not like this."

"There's no promise of tomorrows, Lochlain. We both know that. Why turn your back on love today?" Gwen yelled back, as more Domnua poured forth.

"All right, you crazy woman," Loch finally caved. "Enchantress and sea fairy of mine – I love you and you can battle with me."

Gwen grinned in delight. "I love you," she called, then gasped when she realized she was being separated from the other three by a river of Domnua. A winged dragon broke through the barrier, of such magnitude it made Gwen's heart stop. Hundreds of Domnua rode on its back, and Gwen screamed, realizing she was now isolated from her friends, her team, and her love.

She watched in horror as the dragon blew a magick spell from its mouth, unlike any she had ever heard of, encasing her friends and lover in perfect pillars of ice and shaking the mountain they stood on until it rumbled in anger, lava bursting in waves from the top. Gwen lost sight of her friends, her eyes desperately trying to track where they fell into the water below, before she slid into the black, landing with such an impact that stars stunned her eyes and darkness overcame her.

CHAPTER 40

Gwen blinked, her eyes struggling to adjust to the darkness around her, the only light a faint glow coming from somewhere she couldn't identify to help her to see. She gasped as the ground beneath her shook again. Scrambling to her feet, she realized she'd fallen into some sort of hole or cavern inside the mountain. The sounds of a thousand Domnua screaming aboveground, desperately trying to get to her, propelled her forward.

Feeling her way along the wall, she stumbled forward, the warm glow beckoning her. Realizing she was in a tunnel of sorts, she picked her way further into the mountain, tears running down her face as she tried to not relive the moment that her friends and her love had been blown off the side of the mountain.

"On my life, I swear I will avenge you all," Gwen seethed. She used her bare hands to tear away the rocks in her path, sweat dripping down her face as she drew closer to where the light was, which now shone brighter. Rounding a corner, Gwen skidded to a stop, her hands on her knees, her chest heaving in pain and frustration as tears and sweat ran down her face.

The Spear of Lugh, encased in something that looked like crystal, glowed brightly before her.

"Oh… oh please, please, I need you now," Gwen begged, racing forward to bang her hands on what proved to be a huge block of ice. From inside, the fiery tip glowed a furious red, and Gwen remembered the stories of how the spear had to be encased in cool water or ice lest it destroy all that was around it.

She also remembered that no battle could be won against the one who wielded it.

Determination creasing her brow, Gwen began to bang at the ice, trying everything in her power to crack it, screaming in frustration when not even a chip of ice broke away. Blood ran down her hands, beneath her bracelets, and she held them up, channeling her inner energy to fire more ice at it, hoping against hope that the block would shatter.

She hit the floor when the daggers of ice bounced off, racketing back at her and almost killing her. Curling into a ball, Gwen sobbed in frustration, her mind going once again to those she loved going over the cliff.

Here was the spear, finally, yet she could do nothing with it to save them – or the world that needed her to do so.

"You swore to avenge them, Gwenith. O Gwenith of the sea fairies, enchantress, siren of the seas, she who dances with fairies," Gwen babbled, almost incoherent in her exhaustion and angst, "you've found love and lost it in a day. What kind of power do you hold after all?"

It slammed into her so quickly that Gwen almost slapped

herself in the head for not remembering what Amynta had made her promise to do.

Crossing her arms across her chest, she closed her eyes and let the blood from the cuts on her hands run down her wrists, staining her shirt above her heart. Looking deep inside, Gwen opened her heart to love – to the love that Loch had given her, which resided deep inside of her, to the love of her friends, of Gran, even silly little Macgregor – and let it pour through her.

Lifting her chin, she opened her mouth and sang – an ancient song of love, of legends deep, of hearts won, battles fought, and songs sung. It was the song of the sirens, the song of fairies who danced in the sea, the song of her father's people and her mother's people. The music poured from her, thundering through the room, reverberating up the walls and smashing the ice around the spear into a thousand tiny shards.

And still Gwen sang, spear in hand, as she clambered through a hole that had opened in the side of the mountain. She drew fresh air into her lungs as she ascended the highest peak, the spear raised above her head, her song carrying across the land.

Below her, the Domnua screamed in terror at the sight of the spear – they knew no battle could be won against it. Crouching, Gwen sprang and began to stab Domnua after Domnua, singing like a madwoman, delighting when she heard her people in the waves far below match her in song, their voices raising to a thunderous crescendo.

When the dragon fell from the sky and the last of the Domnua in battle plunged to its death, Gwen lowered the spear and bowed her head, weeping for those she'd lost, knowing she would never again have the love she'd known for such a short time.

Looking out at the horizon, she jumped from the peak, her arms spread in a perfect swan dive, and went to join her people.

CHAPTER 41

*T*he cold water swallowed Gwen, pulling her deep, welcoming her home. As the sweat and blood and sorrow washed from her in the salty water of the sea, she let herself hang, craving the mindlessness of nothing, allowing herself to drop further toward the bottom.

Hands gripped her, pulling her from the numbness her mind had sought to block the pain, and pulled her toward the surface. Gwen broke through the water, tears streaming down her face as she gasped for air, not wanting to feel the pain of loss.

"Shh, my child, shh. Do not cry. You've accomplished a great thing this day," Amynta said, effortlessly swimming her daughter toward shore, the spear glowing brightly between them. Careful not to touch the spear, Amynta wrapped an arm around her daughter's waist and helped her to stand as they reached the shore. For the first time, Gwen looked around her, blinking as she saw her people – hundreds of mermaids and mermen, cheering both on land and in the water, their voices surrounding her with their love and support.

"Your people salute you, Gwen," Amynta chided, and Gwen raised the spear in thanks, standing on wobbly legs, trying her best to smile her thanks. But her mind still raced to those she'd lost this day.

"Your queen," Amynta said, her arm still around Gwen's waist, nudging her to bow as a mermaid, silver stars in her hair forming a sparkling crown, glided through the water to stand before her.

"You've performed a great service for your people this day," the queen said, her voice like moonlight shimmering on water. "Perhaps we were wrong to fear a half-breed such as yourself. What you've done here today has taken great steps towards forming a bond with the fae."

"The fae died for you as well this day. Perhaps you should consider the fact that it isn't race against race, but good against evil. We're all in this together," Gwen said, morosely pointing out the loss of Seamus and Loch, not caring if she sounded rude.

The queen looked surprised at being spoken to in such a manner, and Gwen heard her mother inhale sharply. Lowering her head, Gwen waited for what would come next.

"You've made a good point – something which we shall discuss at high council when next we meet. For now, a gift of our thanks," the queen said.

Gwen raised her head to see several mermen swimming something closer to the shore. "I'm not sure..." she said, unable to figure out what was happening.

"Your friends," the queen said, looking quite pleased with herself, and Gwen screamed, racing across the sand as the mermen gently deposited three tubes of ice, her friends stuck inside of each.

"No, no, no," Gwen said, shocked at the sight of their

frozen visages, locked in terror, forever ensconced in ice. What was the point of bringing them to her like this? Was the queen really that cruel?

"What would you do... if I sang out of tune?" Amynta shocked Gwen by crooning the words she'd sung earlier on the boat, her old Joe Cocker favorite, and Gwen realized what she was doing.

Spreading her arms wide, the spear raised to the air, Gwen sang from the depths of her soul, calling on all the magick in all the realms to use her siren's song to break the ice that imprisoned her friends and her one true love.

When the ice shattered and the three sat up as though awakening from a nap, Gwen dropped to her knees in the sand, the spear still in her hand, and sobbed her thanks. Amynta crouched beside her, whispering her love, then disappeared quickly with the rest of the merpeople. Though they knew the others had seen them, they were still a reclusive race and would not let themselves be seen for longer than necessary.

"You've got the spear!" Bianca gasped.

Gwen leapt up, tackling her in the water with laughter and tears, as Bianca dodged the fiery tip of the spear.

"Careful with that thing. I hear it can take down worlds," Bianca said, patting Gwen's back weakly. Gwen laughed through tears as Seamus kissed her right on the mouth before swinging Bianca into a happy jig across the shore, their laughter echoing across from the cliff walls.

"You found it," Loch said.

Gwen turned, beaming at him in joy. "Aye, I did," she said.

"I can't believe you took such a risk," Loch said, getting up and storming away.

Gwen's mouth dropped open. She looked at the spear in her hand, so furious that she hefted it for a moment, testing its weight and contemplating just nailing the stubborn fool in his head. Sighing, she lowered it and took off after him.

They needed to settle this once and for all.

CHAPTER 42

"You have got to be kidding me," Gwen yelled, as the disgruntled Loch continued to storm away from her. "Remind me again why I saved you if you were going to be so ungrateful about it?"

Loch whirled, fury on his handsome face.

"I'm not ungrateful. I'm angry."

"Looks ungrateful to me," Gwen said, hands on her hips as Loch began to pace in front of her.

"You weren't supposed to find the spear. *I* was. You were supposed to be back at the cottage, safe from harm, while I handled everything," Loch fumed.

"Well, newsflash – that's not how it worked out," Gwen said, holding the spear up.

Loch just shook his head and cursed once more.

"You are an absolute idiot to climb the mountain like that and throw yourself into the line of danger. What were you thinking?" Loch asked.

"I'm an idiot? *I'm* an idiot?" Gwen said, pointing to her chest. "I'm not the one who's an idiot. You turn your back on my love, make me feel like absolute shite, run out on me after you take my innocence and proclaim you love me, all because you wanted to save me from harm? And I'm the idiot?"

"Well, yeah," Loch said, shaking his head in confusion. "Wait, don't turn this around on me."

"Oh, I don't have to turn it around on you. It is on you," Gwen said, her temper kicking up. "What made you possibly think any of this was a good idea? The entire point of me being the Seeker is that I have to find the spear. You wouldn't have been able to find it if you tried. And I'm sorry, but you can't just do everything on your own. I know you want to protect the ones you love – but at what cost? You'd give your life to protect me?"

"Of course I would," Loch said automatically.

Gwen slapped her forehead with her free hand. "Have you learned nothing from your father?"

Loch's face turned thunderous.

"Do not speak of him. He loved my mother beyond worlds."

"I understand that, and what he did for her was a very noble thing. But had he not been so quick to fix it for her, perhaps they could have figured out a solution together. You can't just go around throwing yourself blindly into the face of danger to protect those you love. Sometimes you have to trust that you can work it out as partners," Gwen said patiently.

"What, so we both die?" Loch scoffed.

"I'd rather us both die fighting for the same cause than to lose you to your foolishness. Haven't you seen what kind of life that has been for your mother? Why would you do that to me? I've only just found you." Gwen's voice cracked in frustration and tears threatened.

"I… I don't know. It's all I know how to be. It's all I've

learned. I've never had to make choices *with* others. I've been in protection mode for so long," Loch finally admitted, scrubbing a hand over his face in exasperation.

"Well, it can be us now," Gwen said, stepping forward to look up at him. "If you allow it to be. If you choose it to be."

Loch looked down at her and the world hung suspended in his breath. Gwen saw the answer in his eyes, read the love she'd known was there all along, and smiled up at him.

"I choose it to be, O enchantress of my heart," Loch murmured, bringing his lips to hers in a blistering kiss. Gwen held the spear awkwardly away from them, refusing to break contact with him in the kiss that seared their future together.

"You're going to have to let me make choices too, you know," Gwen said when they broke apart. "I have power as well."

Loch sighed and looked down at her bracelets.

"My life is never going to be dull, that's the truth of it."

"Now who would want a dull life? Do you like cats, by the way? I have this awesome cat that would love to live in the fae world." Gwen chattered away as Loch slung an arm over her shoulder, laughing as she told him about Macgregor.

"I see you two have come to an understanding," Seamus said, nodding his head at them as they walked up. He passed cool eyes over Loch, who stepped forward and held out his hand.

"I'm sorry, my friend. You saw what I wasn't able to see. You had every right to call me out," Loch said.

Seamus took his hand. "Just so long as you see why you were being an idiot," he said, and Loch laughed, pulling him in for a quick hug.

"So, now we need to find the boat and deliver the spear," Bianca said cheerfully. They all groaned as they looked at the staggering cliffs around them and realized the boat was anchored on the other side of the island.

"Nobody said this would be easy," Bianca pointed out.

"But it is nice to have a little help from family," Gwen said, turning to point at the rocky outcropping where the yacht was now moored, another gift from her people.

"This mermaid thing is so damn cool," Bianca breathed.

Gwen laughed, pulling her in for another hug. "I'll tell you all about it on the ride."

CHAPTER 43

"You're certain this is where we need to go?" Loch asked once more, directing the yacht toward the cliffs that jutted out from the coast of western Ireland. The past two days of ocean passage had been easy and joyous, with stories passed among them, a cooler stocked with fruits and treats from the Isle of Destiny, and the light of love in everyone's eyes.

It had been almost like a little lover's cruise, and Gwen found herself barely able to hold back a grin every time she looked at Loch. Maybe the geeky gamer girl did get to win the heart of the handsome superhero every once in a while. Loch took great delight, though, in showing her that she was quite powerful in her own right, and she was slowly growing more confident in herself, both in and out of the bedroom.

"I mean, maybe not, but the last two were directed to Grace's Cove to give the Goddess Danu the treasures for safekeeping." Bianca shrugged.

Loch had grown quieter and more tense the closer they'd gotten to the cove. Last night, Gwen had finally used her wiles to charm the full story out of him, about the sacred blood he'd stolen to save his mother. When she'd related the story to Seamus and Bianca they'd all agreed that there was no way the goddess would still punish him after the courage he'd shown in putting his life on the line for his people.

But Loch just shrugged. "A sacred law is a sacred law."

Which did little for Gwen's anxiety as they approached the cove. She wasn't exactly sure what she would do if the goddess took Loch's life as punishment, after all they had just been through.

"It's lovely, it is," Gwen admitted as they turned the boat into the narrow opening of the cove, the high walls instantly enveloping them as though two arms hugged them – or strangled them, depending on the visitor, Gwen thought, already feeling the press of magick against her skin.

She waited while Bianca performed some sort of offering ritual, which she insisted on doing before she would allow the boat to go any further. When they finally dropped anchor and launched the dinghy on the water, Gwen paused to lay her hand on Loch's arm.

"No matter what happens, I want you to know that I've got your back. I love you and always will," Gwen said.

Loch smiled at her, brushing the softest of kisses over her lips. "My love lives in you, no matter what may come," Loch whispered against her mouth, and Gwen felt her heart skip at the words. Spear in hand, she let the others row the dinghy to shore, her mind furiously working angles to try and circumvent what she was terrified would now happen.

If she understood the power of the spear correctly, no one could win a battle against the person who wielded it. And that included a goddess – or so Gwen hoped.

"Now what?" Gwen asked when they all stood on the shore, the water lapping peacefully at the golden sand.

"We wait," Loch said, his face like stone.

They didn't have to wait long, for the goddess appeared quickly, winking into sight as casually as if she were showing up for a picnic, and strolled across the sand.

Gwen had to admit, the Goddess Danu was stunning, an enchantress of all beauty, power shimmering around her. Everyone dropped to their knees, bowing in the presence of greatness.

Except Gwen.

Instead, she strode forward while Loch cursed from behind her. She stood, spear at the ready, her eyes meeting the Goddess Danu's dead on.

The goddess tilted her head, raising one perfect eyebrow in surprise at Gwen's audacity.

"You don't get to take Loch's life. I don't care what he's done. He's earned the right to stay," Gwen bit out, the spear holding steady as she stared the goddess down.

"Gwen, you can't do that," Loch hissed from behind her.

"I can and will. You've paid your dues. You're an honorable man. I won't allow it," Gwen said, her gaze never breaking contact with the goddess's. The moment held and not a soul on the beach drew a breath. The wind was still, even the water froze in place, as the cove waited with bated breath to see what the goddess would do.

She smiled.

"You've found yourself a worthy mate, Lochlain," Goddess Danu finally spoke, inclining her head barely an inch. "I approve. And though you did not phrase it as a request, I'll take it as such."

"It wasn't –" Gwen began, but Loch cut her off.

"It was a request on my behalf, by my beloved," Loch said, his head bowed.

"And one that I will honor, for great courage was shown by not only herself, but you and your friends as well. I think you've also learned your lesson about love, haven't you, Loch?"

Loch's eyes gleamed as he measured Danu.

"I understand that it isn't a one-way street, my goddess."

"Good. I'm grateful this worked out the way I intended, then. Thank you for your service," Goddess Danu said, and held out her hand for the spear.

Gwen held her eyes for a moment longer, before relinquishing the spear, causing the goddess to throw back her head and laugh.

"Oh, Lochlain, I will delight in watching your life with this one. Many blessings to you both." With that, she winked from sight, the spear gone with her.

Gwen almost collapsed in the sand, her body shaking.

"I'm marrying a crazy woman," Loch decided, looking down at where she trembled at his side.

"Marrying?" Gwen asked, looking up at him with love.

"Well, what did you think this was?" Loch asked, bending to kiss her, and Seamus and Bianca both laughed with delight when the cove glowed a brilliant blue from within, the light rising up to shine on the lovers' shoulders.

The goddess smiled down at them from above, a bit wistfully – for she had always liked Lochlain. But, as she'd always known, he wasn't for her.

But just like the spear she now held, love always found its mark.

*L*ight danced from the shimmering lanterns that hung suspended by magick in the trees, looking for all the world like someone had flung diamonds into the branches. The fae did love glitter, Gwen thought, as she smiled at a woman who danced by, crowning everyone she passed in strands of purple crystals.

"I don't know how I'll ever go back to normal life," Gran said from where she sat next to Gwen, sipping a tea spiked with whiskey, her cheeks rosy with alcohol and joy.

"You might not have to," Loch said, leaning forward to squeeze her hand. "You're welcome in our village, as you've provided a great service to our people by caring so well for Gwen. Had it not been for you protecting her all these years, we'd have lost one of our best Seekers."

Gwen beamed at his praise and then turned to wrap an arm around her gran.

"Do you think you'd like it here? Could you be happy leaving your home? I know how much you love your house, and you've been in the village forever."

Gran paused, considering her words carefully, as she gazed out to where glittering fae danced joyously around a bonfire that was charmed with magick to shift and shimmer with all the colors of the rainbow.

"Aye, I could. I stayed in the village because consistency brought me comfort and, in some small way, I felt as though I could still be near my Henry. But this?" Gran gestured to where magickal fireworks popped in the sky above them. "I'd be a fool to go back to living a life with no magick. Just think of all the beautiful things I can learn and experience. Aye, it's time for me to move on, especially as it will mean I'll be closer to you."

Gwen had agreed that it would be best if she lived with Loch in the fae village in the hills, as it wouldn't make sense for them to hide their powers in her little hometown. If anything, it would make her home more of a target, for – as much as they celebrated this night – the battle was still not yet won.

"I'll feel better knowing you are here – safe." Gwen agreed.

"Will you miss your shop?" Loch asked Gwen, leaning back to pull her to his side, and Gwen almost sighed in delirious delight at the joy that sang through her when she nestled into his arms.

"Oh? The horribly named This & That?" Gwen turned to arch a brow at Loch and he threw back his head and laughed.

"I'm certain you could find a better name together," Gran interrupted and Gwen looked at her in shock.

"You didn't like the name either? You never said a word!" Gwen exclaimed, feeling annoyed that everyone around her seemed to hate her shop name.

"You were so delighted with it, I figured what was the

harm in leaving it be?" Gran shrugged, a little wobbly from the whiskey, and patted Gwen's hand. "I'm sure you could come up with something better if you put your mind to it."

"Hmpf," Gwen said and Loch's body shook with laughter next to hers. She poked his ribs, but found herself chuckling anyway.

"We'll get you a shop space in the village here, my love. The fae will be delighted in being able to buy all sorts of human stuff that they have no need for. It will be the oddity of it all that will draw them. You'll be a hit."

"I can open a shop here?" Gwen squealed, wrapping her arms around Loch in a tight hug.

"You can do anything you want. Except name it This & That," Loch said, and Gwen groaned.

"Fine, fine. You all win. I'll pick a new name," Gwen said, her brain already churning with ideas. She couldn't wait to design a new space.

"I can't believe that Macgregor of yours is soaking this all up. Would you just look at that fat cat?" Gran demanded.

Macgregor, clearly delighting in the fact that fae adored cats, was reclined on a velvet pillow, batting a sparkly poof ball that was magickally suspended above him, while a fae rubbed his belly. He looked for all the world like a fat king with a harem of beauties surrounding him to attend to his every need.

"I have to say – this may be my favorite part of coming to the fae village. Just look how happy he is!" Gwen laughed, delighted with the world in general, raising a glass to toast Bianca and Seamus. Bianca was tugging Seamus away from the fire and Gwen had just the idea of where they were slipping off to. Which was exactly where she would be taking Loch as soon as Gran succumbed to sleep.

"Oh? Really? Your favorite part of being here is making Macgregor happy?" Loch said, sounding a bit miffed.

Gwen smiled up at him. "I suppose there's a few other things... you know, this and that."

She squealed as Loch tickled her ribs, her laughter carrying over the hills to where Amynta floated in the water, her eyes following the revelry with joy.

"Amynta."

Amynta turned, already knowing who said her name. She'd felt him as soon as he'd arrived on the boat near where she'd swum, their love a magnet, forever drawing them to each other.

"Miach."

"Our daughter... she is beautiful," Miach said, inclining forward so that his arms crossed on the side of the boat. Amynta went to him, as she had so many years before, and tilted her head upward.

"Aye, she is at that. We made the right choice, my love," Amynta said, and Miach bent, caressing her face with his hands, and brushed a gentle kiss upon her lips.

"I hold you always in my heart," Miach whispered against her lips.

"I too... for you," Amynta whispered and pulled back, slipping back beneath the water and swimming deep into the darkness. There was nothing more to be said – nothing more that could be done. They both lived in separate worlds and a stolen moment would never ease the pain of longing that Amynta still held deep within her.

Surfacing far away, the fire but a glint on the horizon, Amynta whispered a spell of magick and blessing, sending her love and power across the water to those she loved.

Though she couldn't protect them always, for this one night she would.

For the toughest part was yet to come – both for her world and theirs.

The dramatic and heartwarming conclusion to The Isle of
Destiny Series- Available now as an e-book, paperback or
audiobook!

Sign up for information on new releases, free books, and
fun giveaways at my website www.triciaomalley.com

The following is an excerpt from Sphere Song

Book 4 in The Isle of Destiny Series

CHAPTER 1

"Sister."

The goddess Danu opened her eyes to see her sister, Domnu, Goddess of the Underworld and leader of the dark fae who were currently wreaking havoc on the peaceful world that Danu oversaw. Danu wondered briefly if it would always be this way – the sibling rivalry – if the years in darkness had led Domnu to become a twisted version of the sister Danu had once known.

"Sister," Danu said, inclining her head briefly before standing, her shoulders thrown back, her gaze hard as she measured what her sister had become.

Domnu was dark to Danu's light – no less beautiful, but so very much colder. Where humans would weep in joy at the sight of Danu's purest form – should she ever allow herself to be fully seen by a human – they would be strangely intoxicated by Domnu's dark beauty. Her sinuous aura beckoned, promising a sweet ecstasy, but only in exchange for one bite of the apple. If anything, Domnu had become more beautiful with every evil she'd implemented from being a fierce and unrepentant ruler. It was as if Danu were looking at an icicle, with a cold, crystalline beauty and the sharpest of points that could pierce a warm heart without a thought.

They circled each other, each keenly aware of the other's powers, each unsure of the other's next move. Held here, in this in-between space relegated to the most powerful of beings, they paced. Seeking truths or seeking power, Danu wondered briefly, but held her tongue, waiting for her sister to explain why she'd sought her out. Not that Domnu had tried a usual route – like sending a messenger. Instead, she'd all but ambushed Danu as Danu had worked to sneak through the middle world to find safe haven in a lighter realm.

Safe haven for the treasures she carried, that is, not for herself.

Distinctly aware that the fate of the world as both her fae and humans knew it rested solely in the treasures she had tucked in a chainmail pouch beneath her cloak, Danu refused to blink, her eyes tracking Domnu's every move.

"I'm surprised you'd come here – to this in-between place," Domnu purred, the length of her dark hair seeming to coil and twist of its own accord around her shoulders.

"It's the only way," Danu shrugged, not finishing the thought. For Danu to move the treasures to a safer world, she must first pass through the middle realm. One in which many dangers lay, including her sister. Danu had expected it, was prepared for it, and now she waited to see what would happen.

"You're foolish," Domnu said, her dark eyes snapping in anger and perhaps even disappointment. Did she think Danu had made it too easy for her? "To risk losing the treasures – to open the doors to my people? I'd almost think you'd planned this, or had a reason behind it. Except you never were that dark – were you? It's why, when the worlds split, you went to the light and I went to the dark. It was always in me, you see?"

"Yes, I know," Danu said, somewhat surprised to find that even after all these centuries, it still saddened her. "But there was also good in you. We all have duality, both humans and gods alike. It's what side you let win."

"Let win?" Domnu threw her head back and laughed, the sound like a glass shattering in a million pieces on the floor. "I didn't let it win. I embraced it. Don't you see, my pretty sister? Nothing is more important than what I want. I chose my destiny and now I will decide yours."

Danu blocked the first spell Domnu flung at her – not that she'd put much oomph into it anyway. She was testing her strength, trying to see if Danu would use dark magick to protect herself.

Understanding that it was futile, but still wanting to try, Danu sought to appeal to the light still buried deep within Domnu. "Sister, I see the light in you. It's still there. I know you've enjoyed your reign of terror, but this – this curse, these treasures, the future of our worlds? It will change the history of mankind and fae alike. Kingdoms will fall; magickal beings of all kinds will rape, pillage, and battle. There will be no order, no natural way of being. Even you, my dear sister, will be subject to attack from those wishing to dethrone you. Don't you understand that to allow this to happen – to force it, even – will unleash utter chaos in all the realms as we know them?" Danu said, her eyes never leaving Domnu's.

When she saw the spark of madness deep within the dark depths of her sister's gaze, Danu knew all was lost.

"Chaos breeds change. It's a necessary evil, and change,

my sweet sister, is the only thing we can rely upon," Domnu said, her smile growing wider, maniacal, against the sharp angles of her face.

"You can choose. To be different, to live differently, to rule differently. None of this is necessary," Danu said, circling.

"My people would never forgive me. If it isn't me who leads them to a new world, then it will be another ruler. I refuse to let anyone, even you, stop me," Domnu hissed, and Danu knew the time for conversation was over. She had a half-second to throw her arms up and block herself from the wave of spells that Domnu began drowning her in.

Lightning bolts flashed. They battled, matching spell for spell, light magick clashing against dark. The skies rumbled and time seemed to stop, held on a gasp of breath, as the world waited for what would come next.

And when Danu fell, the treasures torn from her side, she worked the last spell she'd brought with her – the only one that could save them all – and prayed it would do as it was meant. For Domnu planned to take the treasures to the under-world, along with the Seekers themselves.

Danu slitted her eyes open, her energy drained beyond belief, to see Domnu raging as she raced away, dark magick surrounding her as she tried spell after spell to break Danu's light. When she couldn't, she turned to scream at Danu.

"If I can't take them with me, then I'll lock them away until time runs out and the walls to the worlds crumble. You. Will. Not. Stop. Me!"

Domnu winked from sight and Danu closed her eyes, then worked a spell of light and love, whisking it down to her Seekers along with a prayer.

"I'm sorry, my Seekers. It's the only way the last treasure

can be found..." Danu whispered, her hand clutched to her chest as she watched the women she'd come to admire so much being torn from their beds in the middle of the night and ripped away, the dark magick surrounding them before any had a chance to fight it. Only one protector, Lochlain, was able to put a dent in the spell, and it was enough to track his Seeker. For now, the Na Cosantoir would have to stand once more on their own.

Available in audio, e-book & paperback!

Available from Amazon

MS. BITCH

FINDING HAPPINESS IS THE BEST
REVENGE

**Available as an e-book, Hardback, Paperback, Audio or
Large Print.
Read Today**

New from Tricia O'Malley

From the outside, it seems thirty-six-year-old Tess Campbell has it all. A happy marriage, a successful career as a novelist, and an exciting cross-country move ahead. Tess has always played by the rules and it seems like life is good.

Except it's not. Life is a bitch. And suddenly so is Tess.

"Ms. Bitch is sunshine in a book! An uplifting story of fighting your way through heartbreak and making your own version of happily-ever-after."
~Ann Charles, USA Today Bestselling Author of the Deadwood Mystery Series

"Authentic and relatable, Ms. Bitch packs an emotional punch. By the end, I was crying happy tears and ready to pack my bags in search of my best life."
-Annabel Chase, author of the Starry Hollow Witches series

"It's easy to be brave when you have a lot of support in your life, but it takes a special kind of courage to forge a new path when you're alone. Tess is the heroine I hope I'll be if my life ever crumbles down around me. Ms. Bitch is a journey of determination, a study in self-love, and a hope for second chances. I could not put it down!"
-Renee George, USA Today Bestselling Author of the Nora Black Midlife Psychic Mysteries

"I don't know where to start listing all the reasons why you should read this book. It's empowering. It's fierce. It's about loving yourself enough to build the life you want. It

was honest, and raw, and real and I just...loved it so much!"

– Sara Wylde, author of Fat

AFTERWORD

Be sure to check out my website at www.triciaomalley.com. From here you can also sign up to my newsletter for information on new releases, fun giveaways and updates on my Island life!

As always, thank you for your support.

Please consider leaving a review! A book can live or die by the reviews alone. It means a lot to an author to receive reviews, and I greatly appreciate it!

THE MYSTIC COVE SERIES

ALSO BY TRICIA O'MALLEY

Wild Irish Roots (Novella, Prequel)

Wild Irish Heart

Wild Irish Eyes

Wild Irish Soul

Wild Irish Rebel

Wild Irish Roots: Margaret & Sean

Wild Irish Witch

Wild Irish Grace

Wild Irish Dreamer

Wild Irish Sage

Available in audio, e-book & paperback!

Available from Amazon

"I have read thousands of books and a fair percentage have been romances. Until I read Wild Irish Heart, I never had a book actually make me believe in love."- Amazon Review

THE ISLE OF DESTINY SERIES

ALSO BY TRICIA O'MALLEY

Stone Song

Sword Song

Spear Song

Sphere Song

Available in audio, e-book & paperback!

Available from Amazon

"Love this series. I will read this multiple times. Keeps you on the edge of your seat. It has action, excitement and romance all in one series."- Amazon Review

THE SIREN ISLAND SERIES

ALSO BY TRICIA O'MALLEY

Good Girl

Up to No Good

A Good Chance

Good Moon Rising

To Good To Be True

Available in audio, e-book & paperback!

Available from Amazon

"Love her books and was excited for a totally new and different one! Once again, she did NOT disappoint! Magical in multiple ways and on multiple levels. Her writing style, while similar to that of Nora Roberts, kicks it up a notch!! I want to visit that island, stay in the B&B and meet the gals who run it! The characters are THAT real!!!" - Amazon Review

THE ALTHEA ROSE SERIES

ALSO BY TRICIA O'MALLEY

One Tequila

Tequila for Two

Tequila Will Kill Ya (Novella)

Three Tequilas

Tequila Shots & Valentine Knots (Novella)

Tequila Four

A Fifth of Tequila

A Sixer of Tequila

Seven Deadly Tequilas

Available in audio, e-book & paperback!

Available from Amazon

"Not my usual genre but couldn't resist the Florida Keys setting. I was hooked from the first page. A fun read with just the right amount of crazy! Will definitely follow this series."- Amazon Review

AUTHOR'S NOTE

I'm honored that you have taken a chance on my stories – I love writing about Ireland so much – I couldn't help but start a spin-off series.

Thank you for taking part in my world, I hope that you enjoy it.

Please consider leaving a review online. It helps other readers to take a chance on my stories.

As always, you can reach me at
info@triciaomalley.com
or feel free to visit my website at
www.triciaomalley.com.

AUTHOR'S ACKNOWLEDGEMENT

First, and foremost, I'd like to thank my family and friends for their constant support, advice, and ideas. You've all proven to make a difference on my path. And, to my beta readers, I love you for all of your support and fascinating feedback!

And last, but never least, my two constant companions as I struggle through words on my computer each day - Briggs and Blue.